CHRIS SORENSEN

Harmful Monkey Press / Sparta, NJ

Chris Sorensen — First Edition

ISBN 978-0-9983424-5-0

For George Romero, Tom Savini, Rick Baker,
John Carpenter, Don Coscarelli,
and Svengoolie

A hint of mud in your beer, greasy noises in your ear.
Nothing's sounding too clear and it's time to go home.

—Steve Rader, "Suckerville"

ONE

Virgil Orr couldn't believe his fucking luck.

To begin with, Bobbi Jo had accepted his proposal. In front of the whole crew down at Guppy's Lanes. Shelia Warfield, who once told him it'd be a cold day in hell before any woman would let him put a ring on it, was made to eat crow.

Guess ol' Satan better buy some long johns, Shelia, 'cause me and Bobbi Jo McKinney just got hitched.

The next bit of good fortune to fall into his lap was the gift of the pontoon boat on which he and his new bride currently honeymooned, a little something from his Uncle Tuck. Sure, it was over thirty years old and the upholstery was pocked with cigarette burns—Uncle Tuck *loved* his Chesterfields—but a boat was a boat. And Virgil was her new captain.

"What am I doing wrong, pumpkin?" Bobbi Jo asked, lifting her line from the water. For a second, she reminded him of a framed ad his grandfather had hanging on the wall of his basement workshop: a buxom gal in a crop top three sizes too small struggling to land a humungous fish. The caption read: *Keep Your Hands Off My Bass!*

"Lemme see, sweet cheeks."

Virgil threw the engine into neutral, dropped anchor, and picked his way around coolers packed with fried chicken and beer.

Bobbi Jo flipped her ponytail and flashed him a smile as he approached, revealing a sexy snaggletooth. Standing there in the bright June sun, the green Mississippi River stretching out behind her, she looked like a goddess. A snaggletoothed goddess in a Lynyrd Skynyrd T-shirt.

"I lost your lure," she apologized, holding out her fishing pole. Sure enough, the popper was gone, the line bitten clean through.

"No worries," Virgil said, expertly flipping open one of the coolers with a sandaled foot. "Think it's time for us to give my balls a try."

"Virgil!"

With a grin, Virgil squatted down and extracted a Ziploc filled with sticky, brown orbs.

"Wheatie balls, I mean. Catfish go nuts for them."

"The fish go nuts for your balls?"

"They do at that."

Bobbi Jo clucked her tongue. "This I gotta see."

Virgil winked and made a show out of tying a new treble hook to Bobbi Jo's line before mushing one of the Wheatie balls around its shank, hiding the barbs.

"And that's how you do it," he crowed, holding the glistening ball aloft. His new wife applauded gleefully.

"Gimme, gimme!"

She grabbed the pole from Virgil's hands, and their fingers brushed against each other, sending electricity shooting up his arms and down his belly. Sure, it was midday, and they were floating out in the open where any barge captain or speedboat operator had a clear view, but Virgil felt the sudden desire to consummate their marriage right then and there. Not that they hadn't been getting busy ever since that first night after the bowling tournament at Guppy's—theirs was the most passionate lovemaking Virgil had ever known—but the combo of the gentle rocking of the boat and the buzz from the beer had gotten him good and randy.

"Plop that ball in the water and give me a little sugar, sweet cheeks," he said, letting the words rumble around in the back of his throat.

Bobbi Jo laughed at his forced bravado, but it did the trick. She flicked the Wheatie ball into the current and set the rod in the holder before nuzzling up close.

"Right here out in the open, Mr. Orr?" she said in mock protestation.

"Why not, Mrs. Orr?" Virgil replied, moving in for a smooch. But as soon as his mustache hit her upper lip, she recoiled as if she'd just kissed a porcupine.

"You have *got* to shave that damn thing off, Virge."

"You kidding? This here's my pride and joy. It makes me look like Burt Reynolds."

"It makes you look like a porn star."

Virgil grinned. "Bow-chicka-bow-wow," he crooned, attacking her neck and making her squeal.

He cranked the radio—Walker Hayes crooned "Fancy Like," setting the mood. The two frantically peeled off each other's clothing, exposing themselves to the Illinois shore starboard and the Iowa shore port.

"And you *have* to get that removed," Bobbi Jo chided, running her fingers over the badly-drawn pair of dice tattooed on his bicep.

"Anything you say, dear," he dutifully replied as he buried his face in her neck.

The two were blissfully unaware as Bobbi Jo's fishing pole leaped into the water and disappeared. The pale couple coupled on the damp deck, taking no note as the boat's anchor cable went taut, guiding the rocking craft into a narrow inlet that snaked into the woods.

"I love you more than country music. I love you more than my truck," Virgil whispered.

"Oh, Virge!"

"I love you more than—"

"Shut up," Bobbi Jo said, silencing his mouth with her own.

———

By the end of their raucous session, two of the three Styrofoam coolers had been kicked over, and one of Virgil's sandals had made a dive for the water. The radio had moved on to the Zac Brown Band power hour. Bobbi Jo lay panting face down, her fingers still clutching shreds of rotted carpet she'd ripped free from the deck while in the throes of passion.

"Damn, honey," Virgil said, falling back, his heart still pounding in his throat.

"Virge…" Bobbi Jo moaned.

Virgil wiped the sweat from his brow and threw back his head to loose a wolf howl at the sky, but the sky had disappeared. In its place was a ceiling of foliage so thick it blocked out the June sun.

"That's weird."

Virgil glanced about. They were no longer anchored offshore—somehow, the pontoon boat now lay adrift in a dark channel of brackish water. At first, he was glad for the unexpected privacy. Perhaps their seclusion could convince Bobbi Jo to go for round two. But when the boat bucked suddenly, alarm bells went off.

"Virge…"

"Hold on," Virgil said, rising in all his naked glory. He leaned over the edge and took stock of the ripples in the water. What had they just hit? A sunken log? A ginormous snapping turtle? He'd once caught a whopper of a snapper by accident using Wheatie balls, and damned if the thing hadn't come crawling ashore like some armored transport landing on Omaha Beach. It had hissed, its prehistoric jaws snapping like gunfire. The thought of the turtle made Virgil suddenly eager to protect his manhood, and he grabbed up his underwear.

As he yanked up his briefs, something struck the boat hard enough to set it twirling counterclockwise. Virgil tried to maintain his balance, failed, and toppled onto Bobbi Jo's back.

"Sorry, honey. I'm not trying to start nothin', I just… something in the water is playing games with us."

"Virge..."

"Shit, sorry," he said, scrambling off his wife. He held out a hand.

"I can't get up."

"Huh?"

Bobbi Jo pressed her hands against the deck and tried to muster a push-up, but she rose only a few inches before dropping with a cry.

"Jeez, was I too rough?" Virgil asked apologetically. He straddled the naked girl and slid his hand beneath her armpits. "All right. Upsy-daisy."

Virgil lifted, and Bobbi Jo screamed. He let go.

"What the hell, honey?"

Suddenly, the water about the boat began to roil and churn, threatening to toss Virgil overboard. He grabbed the rail and rode the bucking boat like a bronco as chicken wings and beer cans abandoned ship. He looked over at Bobbi Jo— she was still plastered to the deck, legs kicking and arms flailing. And now, the carpet beneath her was turning red. Was that blood?

"Babe!" he shrieked, and at that, the chaos abated. The boat settled into a slow rock as the water went still.

Bobbi Jo jerked once and went still as well.

"Babe?"

Virgil stood shivering in his underwear, mustache wet and drooping like a drowned caterpillar. God. There was so much blood.

"Bobbi Jo?"

The girl took an enormous gulp of air, causing Virgil to shriek again. She wrenched herself from the deck accompanied by twin sucking *pops*. She let out a rasping cough, painting the deck redder still with her spittle.

Virgil's wife rose jerkily, her back to him. Mooning him.

Virgil's eyes dropped to the blood-stained carpet—the deck sported two freshly-made holes as if some cartoon creature had taken a couple of bites out of it.

Bobbi Jo turned.

Her eyes had lost their sparkle and green hue. Now they were milk-white, all trace of her pupils had been eaten away. Her mouth hung open much, *much* too far.

Virgil's attention drifted past his wife's slack jaw to her chest, and for a moment, he heard his mother's voice scolding him, *When you take a girl out, eyes up, you hear me? No gal likes havin' her boobies stared at.*

But he couldn't help but stare. Gone were the nipples he loved to nuzzle. In their place gaped two angry red mouths filled with pinprick teeth.

"Oh, fuck."

Bobbi Jo grinned and staggered toward him, her arms outstretched, her eyes locked on his.

Virgil stood frozen as she embraced him, pulling him close, gurgling in his ear.

Sharp pain erupted in his chest as her mammary-mouths bit down, teeth piercing his flesh and nicking his ribs. A wave of euphoria washed over him, and Virgil thought, *This must be how a fly feels when the spider chomps down.*

He stared into Bobbi Jo's face, marveling how her mouth —her original mouth, not the newly born toothy twins currently sucking him dry—twisted into an O, her jawbone snapping and reconfiguring itself. Blood trickled from her gums as her snaggletooth elongated, sizing up his eyes.

"Bobbi—"

She bit down on his face. Her teeth clicked against his as she ripped away his upper lip, mustache and all, before feasting on his jowls.

Sweet cheeks, he thought, and for the second time that day, Virgil Orr couldn't believe his fucking luck.

TWO

"Speers! Get up!"

The voice so startled JD that he leaped up from the metal bench on which he'd been lying and promptly decorated the cell floor with last night's hot wings. His cellmate, an old fellow in nothing but sweatpants, farted reveille his sleep.

"Jesus Christ," sneered the uniformed man on the other side of the bars. Calvin Drake was a walking advertisement for redneck cops. His buzzcut was as short as his temper. He grabbed a handful of napkins from next to the water cooler, and threw them into the cell. "Clean up that mess. Your mother doesn't work here."

"Yeah, but yours does, Cal. She came to visit me in the middle of the night."

"Shut your trap."

"I said, 'No, Calvin's Mom, no! We can't do this...'"

"I'm warning you."

"But she was real insistent."

The cop slammed the bars with his clipboard, sending

JD's headache into overdrive. But it was worth it to see old Cal so riled up.

"There a problem in there?" came a booming voice from the adjoining room.

"No, Captain," Cal the Cop said.

"Good."

JD rose and approached the bars, careful to stay out of the police officer's reach.

"How's anger management training going, Cal?"

"Shut up."

"You still keeping this town safe from high school kids necking at Muhlberg Park? Still yanking those little bastards from their cars and beating them in front of their dates?"

Cal seemed about ready to strike the bars again but thought better of it. Instead, he counted to three and checked his clipboard. The old fellow on the floor rolled over and cut the cheese again.

"Speers, JD. Public intoxication, criminal mischief..."

"Stop reading my resume and let me out."

"Not so fast." Cal had a boxer's face, broken nose and all, and at this moment, it also sported a rather pleased smile.

"What do you mean?"

"Mr. Stanton down at the bank wants to make an example of you..."

"No, no, no. Wait a minute—"

"And Capt. Mikita concurs. Looks like you picked the wrong Friday night to go swimming in the First Federal water fountain."

"I never..."

JD went silent. An image of himself sitting waist-deep in a pool, jets of water arcing overhead flashed before his eyes, and a sour taste rose in his throat, rebooting his memory.

Oh...damn. Elsie and the frozen margaritas.

Cal saw the penny drop and went in for the kill.

"I hate having to tell Kate about your little rendezvous. You know how your shenanigans pain her. Ah, well...I guess I'll have to break the news to her during our date tonight. I'm taking her to Burlington for steaks."

"To the Big Muddy?" JD asked.

"Yup."

"They make a great steak."

"Sure do." Cal rubbed at his mouth. "But I think we'll go back to my place for dessert."

JD saw red. He suddenly wanted to wipe the stupid grin off Cal's face. It was bad enough his ex-wife would learn about his evening escapades, but to hear it from Cal's mouth? His stupid, smirking mouth?

He was about to make a grab for Cal's throat when a squat woman with tomato-red cheeks poked her head into the room.

"What's he still doing here?" the woman barked.

"Well, Captain, I was just..." Cal stammered.

"He was just telling me how you're going make an example of me, Linda," JD said.

"The man made bail. Let him out," Capt. Mikita ordered, glaring at Cal. "What's wrong with you?"

"Right away, Captain."

"Chop chop!"

"Yes, Captain."

Capt. Mikita stalked out of the room, leaving Cal shaken.

JD rapped on the cell door's lock.

"You heard the woman. Chop chop!"

The fresh air that greeted JD as he exited the Oquawka Police Department was a welcome relief from the fart-haunted cell, but the harsh sunlight was something he could do without. He instinctively reached for his shirt pocket and found it empty. No doubt his sunglasses lay at the bottom of First Federal's water fountain.

"Yo! Jailbird!" a familiar voice called. "Over here."

JD shielded his eyes and squinted. Leaning against a beat-up Chevy pickup parked across the street in front of The Village Pump Grill was Rowdy in all his beer-bellied glory. Sunlight glinted off his enormous American flag belt buckle. His ever-present Bowie knife in its worn leather sheath hung at his waist like an extra appendage. Whiskered and whiskeyed up, Rowdy was a sight for sore eyes.

JD shook his head. "You bailed me out?"

"Of course I did."

"Why?"

"Friends don't give up on friends, that's why."

"How much did that set you back?"

"Enough."

"You know I'm good for it."

"Like hell you are." Rowdy climbed into the truck and revved the engine. "We getting a drink or what?"

Half an hour and four road sodas later, the two were barreling north on Front Street, the sun setting below the Mississippi. Rowdy cranked the radio, and classic Garth filled the air.

JD hung out the passenger side window, aiming a crumped aluminum can at an approaching clawfoot tub sitting in front of a double-wide trailer.

"Five bucks says I make it."

"Make it a six-pack, and you're on."

As they neared the yard with the tub, Rowdy hit the gas. Thrown by the truck's sudden acceleration, JD loosed the can too early, missing his mark by a country mile.

"No fair!" JD cried.

"All's fair in love and beer bets."

"I'm not paying up."

"You never do."

Rowdy was right—he'd never see his bail money or the six-pack. He, JD Speers, was an unreliable man. Always had been; always would be. The realization made him judgmental of the fellow he saw staring back at him in the rearview mirror. The guy had three days' growth on his chin, dark circles under his eyes, and looked vaguely like his father, Roger Speers, a man who died at fifty-five, having spent forty of those years making love to a bottle.

The memory of old Roger prompted JD to fish another beer from the cooler between his feet.

"You want another?" he offered.

"Better not," Rowdy said, waving him off and burping wetly. "It ain't mixing well with the rye. I'll hold off 'til Doc's."

"Suit yourself," JD said, taking a big swig.

They turned onto Route 3 North, and Rowdy promptly passed a slow-moving semi. JD pumped his fist, urging the driver to honk his horn. He didn't.

"So...why the hell was you skinny dipping in the water fountain?"

"Oh, don't even—"

"I paid your bail; you gotta spill."

JD downed another mouthful of the sour swill. "Cindy Beiderbecke said she wanted to take a dip."

"Beiderbecke? Ain't you two related?"

"Barely."

Rowdy rolled his eyes.

"I was lonely, all right? Is that what you want me to say?"

"Everyone's lonely. Hell, I'm lonely, but you don't see me getting thrown in the clink for skinny dipping."

"We had a few margaritas at Mud Daubers, then she said she wanted to take a little romantic swim with me. City pool's closed on account of giardia, so—"

Rowdy swerved off the road. For a moment, JD thought his friend meant to plow headlong into the cornfield flanking the road, but he pulled hard on the wheel and skidded to a stop on the gravel shoulder. Rowdy waited until the cement truck behind them rumbled past, then turned, a solemn look on his face.

"You know what your problem is?"

JD shook his head. "Here we go."

"You're a fuckup. That's your fucking problem."

"Thank you, Dr. Phil."

"I'm serious. You fucked up your marriage, fucked up plenty of jobs. Whatever happened to that hauling gig I got you?"

JD threw his beer out the window, baptizing the corn. "Jerry Jensen is an asshole."

"He said you went AWOL after one day of work. Didn't have a clue where you ran off to."

"Like I said, Jerry is an—"

"You're a good guy, JD. It's just that...you've got no initiative, you never finish nothin' you start, you got a real problem with impulse control, you're—"

"A fuckup."

"In a word, yes."

"Well, fuck you."

"Fuck you right back."

The two men glared at each other a moment before bursting out laughing.

"Look," Rowdy said. "You're a young guy. What are you, thirty-six? Thirty-seven?"

"I'm twenty-eight, Rowdy."

"Really? Twenty-eight?"

"Jesus..."

"Anyway, what I'm tryin' to say is you should leave that lonely talk to broken-down horses like me. And you gotta make better choices, boy. Don't make me bail you out again, you hear me?"

"I hear you."

Rowdy threw the truck into drive and veered back onto the road. "We missed happy hour, but I'm sure Doc will set us up. You still game?"

JD paused as his fuckup mind landed upon a truly interesting, fucked up idea.

"Hey, Rowdy," he said with a grin. "Mind if we take a little detour first?"

THREE

Otis munched on his hidden stash of peanut butter cups as Pastor Jim circled the group of kids, holding the dirty magazine aloft.

"We're not roasting a single weenie until I find out who this filth belongs to," Pastor Jim said, eyeing each and every Bible Scout sitting around the campfire. "Who the heck thought this was appropriate reading material for our Camping with Jesus Weekend?"

The boy sitting to Otis's left snorted, and the wiry pastor in khaki shorts whirled on him.

"Was it you, Mickey Burns?"

"No, Pastor Jim."

The boy to Otis's right flinched.

"You have something to add, Tony Lawson?"

"I've never bought a magazine in my life," Tony said, raising his hands. "I swear."

The rest of the Bible Scouts nodded in agreement as if assuring the scoutmaster that magazines had gone the way of the rotary phone and the dodo. Otis was the lone holdout.

Trying desperately to stifle a chocolatey burp, he failed to join in with his bobble-headed friends. Pastor Jim turned on him like a cat on a mouse.

"Otis!"

The boy blinked as he felt Pastor Jim's gaze fall upon him. The man held the magazine under his nose, a scantily-clad female lumberjack with impossible proportions on the cover.

"You're rather quiet." Pastor Jim bent so close Otis could see the tiny veins pulsing on top of his bald pate.

"I..."

"Yes?"

"I..."

"Spit it out."

"I gotta poo!"

The scouts erupted in laughter. Pastor Jim sneered.

"Go make your toilet, boy."

Otis scurried to his feet.

"You have your biodegradable TP?"

"Yes, sir," Otis said, slipping on his backpack and LED headlamp.

"Good. Don't dawdle."

As Otis traipsed off down the hiking trail, swapping the comfort of the campfire for the darkening woods, he heard Pastor Jim launching into his sermon, his voice a clarion bell in the wilderness.

"The rest of you little perverts open your Bibles. Instead of hot dogs, we're going to feast on the word of the Lord."

By the time Otis was well out of earshot of the rest of the troop, he paused to retrieve a backup magazine from his pack. He'd swiped it from his old man's stash in the garage—his father kept his naughty library in an old cedar chest along with stacks of birthday cards and his high school wrestling outfit.

Otis bowed his head, training the headlight on the magazine. *Community Chest*. The gal on the cover was dressed like Mr. Moneybags from Monopoly. Otis thought she could pass Go anytime she wanted.

"Hubba hubba," Otis said, parroting one of his father's catcalls. His old man was notorious for harassing the female waitstaff at Hooties during their regular Saturday night family outings. His mom despised the place, but it was the happiest Otis saw his dad all week.

He directed his light at the trail ahead and found that the path descended toward a creek, not fifty yards ahead. Good. Better to do his business near water instead of leaving a steaming pile in the woods like an animal.

As Otis trudged on, he realized what he had first mistaken for a creek was instead an inlet of the Mississippi itself. The water lapped against the shoreline like a pack of thirsty dogs.

Upon reaching the water's edge, Otis slipped off his pack, and loudly answered nature's call. A bird high above in the trees twittered its annoyance. When Otis was finished, he rummaged around in his pack for the toilet paper but came up empty.

"Dang."

Improvising, Otis retrieved the magazine, ripped free a page of ads for erectile dysfunction pills, and wiped.

He was about to pull his shorts back up when he spied movement out of the corner of his eye. He stood quickly and glanced about, training his headlamp left and right to catch whatever critter might be out there.

Nothing.

Otis yanked up his shorts and cinched the canvas belt tight. He tossed a few stones into the water, delaying his return back to camp. The stones hit with satisfying *plunks*. Then, he stuffed the magazine into his pack and slipped it over his shoulders, readying for the trip back. But the sound of metal scraping against rock stopped him dead in his tracks.

He crouched behind some brush and tried to douse his headlamp. The switch wasn't working, so he clasped his hand over the light to extinguish its glare.

At first, Otis thought his mind was playing tricks on him, but the longer he watched, the more sure he was of what he saw. Slipping almost silently down the inlet was a battered pontoon boat, one of its pontoons split down the middle like a peeled banana, the weight of the water it had taken on causing the craft to tilt at a dangerous angle.

The boat was a splintered mess. It must have tangled with a barge and floated down this inlet to die. It was hard to see without exposing his headlamp, but try as he might, Otis couldn't make out a single person on board.

They're probably all dead, he thought, and the prospect of possibly seeing such a sight, of gaining the bragging rights of seeing an actual dead body—guts exposed, eyes bulging— made him brave enough to uncover his light.

The scene his headlamp revealed was even more ghastly than he could have imagined. Illuminated in the garish, green-white light, the pontoon boat looked like a crime scene. Blood and gore painted the craft from bow to stern. What looked disturbingly like intestines hung looped around the twisted canopy frame, wet and glistening. Something horrible had happened onboard, the evidence of which was on full, nasty display.

Otis noticed something else, something that caused his knees to lock even though he wanted—no, *needed*—to run.

Someone was climbing out of the mangled boat.

"Hello?" he warbled, his voice shaking, playing the same trick as his knees.

The lone passenger crept out of the clusterfuck of a boat and stood poised on the bow, balancing there with all the agility of a hawk.

But this was no hawk. This was a woman. And she was naked as a jaybird.

"Hubba hubba," Otis said under his breath.

The woman was drenched from head to foot in blood, a fact which made her milky eyes stand out all the more. A fraying ponytail hung down one side of her head, and a wayward incisor jutted from her rows of overly-large teeth. The woman opened her mouth and loosed a guttural growl.

What's up with her boobs?

When a second and third mouth opened where nipples once lived, Otis had his answer.

It was time to *git.*

The terrified Bible Scout forced his legs to move. He tore off down the trail toward camp, screaming his head off. But, having sprinted a mere twenty feet, he discovered that, no... the boat hadn't had only one passenger. No, the naked lady had company.

20

And he was blocking the path.

Otis's headlamp shook violently as he spasmed with fear, the beam of light zipping back and forth across the trail. The man with the split belly and blood-soaked undies ducked in and out of the light. He was ten feet away...no, three. Before Otis could make his escape, the man was upon him, his mouth twisting into a rasping oval of razor-sharp teeth.

As the man bit down, relieving the boy's shoulder of its flesh, Otis thought...

He smells like hamburger meat.

Pastor Jim had the scouts' rapt attention. Or rather, the ventriloquist dummy on his knee with the long beard and satin robe had their attention. The boys stared open-mouthed in a mix of wonder and dismay.

The scoutmaster had obviously carved the puppet himself. Its head was too big for its body, and its facial features were chiseled all out of proportion, causing it to more resemble the Elephant Man than the Son of God.

"What was that you said, Jesus?" Pastor Jim asked in an enthusiastic entertainer's voice.

The Jesus puppet clapped its mouth open and closed like a carp and screeched, "I said that if you do not obey me, then you will eat the flesh of your sons and daughters. I will pile your dead bodies on the lifeless forms of your idols. Leviticus 26:27."

Pastor Jim nodded thoughtfully. "Words to live by, Jesus. Words to live by."

"Hey, boys!" the Jesus puppet shouted. "Let's sing a song. How about, 'This Little Light of Mine!'"

The troop had just launched into the first verse when the flickering light of an approaching lamp illuminated the trees about them.

Otis stumbled into camp.

"That must have been some major BM, dude," Tony Lawson snorted.

"What, didja fall in?" Mickey Burns cried.

Otis stepped into the light of the fire, and from his appearance, it did indeed look as if he had fallen in. His uniform was shredded, and his hair stuck out wildly to the side, plastered with mud. Dark liquid trickled from the corners of his mouth, and his eyes were as pale as a fish's belly.

He also had a monster-sized hickey on his neck. And it was gushing blood.

"Otis, where have you been?" Pastor Jim said, scowling. "You missed Jesus's opening prayer. As your penance, you're going to lead the New Testament reading. Open your Bibles to...to..."

The scoutmaster fell silent as Otis opened not his Bible but his mouth. The boy's jaw unhinged unceremoniously as his gums pressed outward, inflamed like a baboon's hindquarters. A thicket of teeth pierced flesh, flexing in a deadly circle of hunger.

Pastor Jim thrust forward the dummy like a talisman as the boy approached.

"Begone, Satan!" Jesus shrieked.

Otis howled and leaped over the campfire, striking coals with his feet and scattering them into the laps of the horrified scouts. In a single, swift move, the boy clamped his entire mouth over the dummy's head and bit down hard. The puppet's wooden noggin splintered in Otis's jaws, and the boy pulled back, confused.

"Sinner!" Pastor Jim hissed.

Otis turned from the dummy to the man and, with the prepubescent screams of his fellow scouts echoing in his ears, sank his teeth deep into the pastor's face.

FOUR

"In the realm of bad ideas," Rowdy said, "this is *way* the fuck up there. Didn't you hear a word I said about making better choices?"

The old aircraft-style Airstream parked alongside Kate's modest cabin glowed orange in the setting sun. The hulking metal beast reminded JD of Norma Jean, the circus elephant that had come to town only to be struck down by lighting. The circus had buried the poor animal in the Oquawka dirt and moved on, leaving a small plaque to mark her passing. The Airstream looked as dead as that elephant, and it didn't even get a plaque.

"This is a good choice, Rowdy. It's a *real* good choice."

"By what twisted logic do you come to that conclusion?"

JD turned to his friend. "You called me a fuckup."

"I did."

"Well, what man wouldn't be a fuckup without a place to hang his hat? You know what they say: a man's home is his castle. Without a castle, what the hell am I?"

"Where are you going with this, your highness?" Rowdy grumbled.

"I've got nothing. Kate took everything when she left. *Everything.* My confidence, my reason for living, my hot tub. And the real kicker? She took my damn Airstream."

"Okay..."

"That camper and I were in a relationship long before I met Kate. Hell, I lived in it for two years up in the Black Hills when I was flipping bison burgers and then again when I worked that snake farm down in Kissimmee."

"I liked that snake jerky you sent for Christmas."

"That Airstream is mine."

Rowdy wrinkled his brow. "Then how come it's sitting in her yard?"

JD threw up his hands. "Because my lawyer ended up being her second cousin, and I didn't find that out until it was too late."

"I thought it was 'cause you racked up a couple thousand on her credit cards—"

"Stop interrupting my train of thought! As I see it, a man's entitled to what's his. And if he doesn't make a stand, you know...if man doesn't stand, what is he?"

"A cripple?"

"No! Jesus, Rowdy."

A car passed behind them on the sandy road, and both men ducked down until it had disappeared from view.

Rowdy put his hand on JD's shoulder. "This ain't about the camper."

"Sure, it is."

"It's about Kate, and you know it. You gotta forget about her. She's a dental hygienist now. She's gone."

JD stared at the Airstream and let out a deep breath. "She's not even using it. It's just sitting there like an old boot."

"I hear you."

"Rowdy?"

"Yeah?"

"I want my boot back."

<hr />

JD guided the pickup back toward the camper. Rowdy was doing his best to stay on target, but he was flying blind without towing mirrors.

JD had tried to open the Airstream's door and windows, but like his ex's legs during the final few years of their marriage, they were locked up tight.

"How much farther?" Rowdy shouted.

"Six feet. Five..."

"You sure she ain't coming home any time soon?"

"Not a chance. Ol' Cal the Cop is taking her to Burlington for steaks."

"To the Big Muddy?"

"Yup."

"They make a great steak—"

"Stop!"

Rowdy slammed on the brakes, coupler lined up perfectly with the camper's ball hitch. JD took it as a sign. The planets were aligning; the universe meant for him to have his Airstream back.

"Oh, shit..." Rowdy whispered.

JD looked at Rowdy—the man's face had gone white. He

followed his friend's gaze and landed upon a figure dressed in green scrubs standing on the cabin's front porch.

Kate was home. And she was gripping a double-barreled shotgun.

"You sonofabitch!" she spat.

She leveled the gun and fired. The blast hit the Airstream, pellets ricocheting every which way. A couple clipped JD's ear, and white-hot pain erupted.

"What the hell, Kate?" he screamed.

"You thieves! You goddamn bums!" She took aim again and let off another shot. This time, she missed JD, hitting Rowdy's truck instead.

"I didn't sign up for this!" Rowdy roared, revving the engine.

"Wait up!" JD shouted.

Kate advanced, reloading as she did.

"You're supposed to be on a date!" JD cried, frantically hooking the trailer to the pickup.

"I had to change first!"

"You're looking good. Did you get your hair cut?"

"Fuck you, JD!"

Kate let off another shot. The pickup's rear window exploded.

"Train's leaving the station!" Rowdy shouted and threw the truck into gear.

The Airstream jerked forward, lurching over its chocks and nearly crushing JD in the process. He jumped aboard the hitch and grabbed hold of the pickup's tailgate. The camper fishtailed with the sudden acceleration, taking out a bird-bath and a mirrored gazing ball.

The next shot hit the back of the camper as they sped

away, and JD heard Kate dropping f-bombs like a sailor, but the hard part was over.

He'd gotten his boot back.

JD lurched into the truck bed and clambered through the hole where the rear window used to be.

Rowdy pulled a wad of napkins from under the dash and tossed them to JD.

"Staunch that wound, son. You'll bleed all over my truck."

"Sorry," JD said, pressing the napkins to his bloodied earlobe, feeling it burn.

"You know we're doing time for this, right?" Rowdy fumed.

"How do you mean?"

"Oh, I don't know! We just absconded with your ex's camper—"

"*My* camper."

"Not in the eyes of the law, it ain't. And she's got a date with a member of law enforcement this very night. I'm thinking there's a chance it might come up in conversation, how about you?"

JD pondered this. "So you're saying this is one of those impulse control things."

"I'm saying this is nuts!"

The pickup veered left off the main road and down a long drive flanked on either side by pine trees, the Airstream's tires screeching angrily.

"What are you doing?" JD asked.

"Taking to the woods. I wanna lay low until I can wrap my head around this situation."

"Maybe she'll forgive and forget. Stranger things have happened."

Rowdy let out an incredulous laugh. "Forgive? Forget? She blasted us with buckshot, boy. If anything, she's rounding up a posse as we speak."

An electronic bleep sounded from JD's crotch. He ditched the soaked napkins out the window and fished the phone from his pocket.

"Kate's texting."

"What's she say?"

JD read the message on the screen. "You're dead."

"I knew it. I fucking knew it."

"She's saying *I'm* dead. Doesn't say anything about you."

"I'm your damned accomplice! Without me and my truck, that camper's still sitting alongside her house."

"I guess you're right."

"Damn right, I'm right!"

They passed a faded wooden sign that read *Delabar State Park* and rumbled past a sparsely-populated campground—a few tents, a couple of campers, the glow of joints being passed around campfires. As the sun bid its farewell, Rowdy took a side road, leaving the campground and civilization behind.

Rowdy flicked on the headlights. The road turned to dirt and rock as they drew closer to the river. It dipped in places, causing the truck's undercarriage to scrape bottom. Rowdy grimaced as if feeling it in his nuts. A buckshot sign read, *Narrow Road – 1 Mile*. The shoulder on JD's side encroached as the road wound its way through swampy terrain. A couple of feet to the right and into the muck they'd drop.

"Sorry I dragged you into this," JD said.

Rowdy glanced at him sideways. "Hell, I don't get dragged nowhere I don't wanna go. You know that."

"Still..."

"Apology accepted. Why don't you pass me one of those beers."

JD reached into the cooler. "They're warm."

"Beer me all the same."

JD grabbed a lukewarm can for Rowdy and one for himself. His buddy skillfully cracked his suds single-handed while still managing to avoid a rock in the road.

"Guess we're both fuckups," Rowdy said, raising his beer. "To fuckups."

"To fuckups."

As the men toasted each other, the truck hit a deep rut in the road. Rowdy's beer slipped from his grasp and plummeted to the floor.

"Dammit!" Rowdy shouted. "Take the wheel."

JD quickly grabbed the steering wheel with his free hand as his buddy rooted around below, searching for his wayward brewsky. All JD had to do was to keep them driving straight. No worries. He took a sip of his suds while Rowdy rooted around for his beer.

Something darted in front of the truck, momentarily illuminated by the glare of the pickup's headlights.

What the hell?

Whatever it was moved too quickly for JD to get a good look, but not fast enough to get out of their way.

"Brakes. Brakes!" JD cried, bracing for impact. A second later, it came. Metal struck bone, and the pickup hopped as it crushed something beneath its wheels.

Rowdy popped up. "What just happened?"

"I think we hit something."

"Fuck!" Rowdy cried, grabbing control of the wheel.

Rowdy mashed the brake pedal to the floor, but with the camper's forward momentum, the pickup barely slowed.

Oncoming headlights flooded the cabin.

"Fu-u-uck!"

JD's stomach dropped. Just his dumb fucking luck. A damn car was heading straight toward them. They were barreling headfirst toward the other vehicle with seven thousand unstoppable pounds of Airstream riding their ass.

FIVE

T he two vehicles struck with the force of twin runaway trains meeting on the same track, sending both men in the pickup hurtling through the windshield, shredding them like so much pulled pork.

Or...at least that's the scenario JD's brain conjured up in the split seconds before Rowdy spun the steering wheel with all the dexterity of an Indy 500 driver. The pickup skidded sideways, the truck and car missing each other by inches.

The Airstream's fate was a different matter. Having been rudely yanked to the left by the pickup, it responded by jack-knifing. The approaching car swerved in an attempt to avoid a direct hit, but the camper was just too big of a target to miss. JD felt the *crunch* as the other vehicle struck the Airstream.

Rowdy stomped on the parking brake, and the truck-trailer combo came to a shuddering stop.

"Holy shit," Rowdy said, knuckles white from gripping the wheel.

JD turned to the rearview mirror but it was gone, having been blasted away by his ex.

"Holy shit," Rowdy repeated.

"I'm going to go check things out." JD hopped out of the truck. "You okay?"

"Holy—"

"Shit. Yeah, I hear you. Be right back."

JD took a quick glance at the front of the pickup and instantly regretted it.

When he was eight, his brother Beane had hit a deer while driving them home from a movie in the Quad Cities. The viscera that coated the front of Rowdy's truck reminded JD of that unfortunate deer's remains.

Whatever creature had tested its luck crossing the road had lost, leaving bits and pieces behind. A swath of dark blood painted the hood; clumps of hair and flesh stuck in the grill. It had taken Beane days to rid his car of the deer's gore; it would take Rowdy weeks.

"Was it a deer?" Rowdy called out the window. JD thought he sounded desperate for a 'yes.'

"That's what I'm guessing." Although the moment it was out of JD's mouth, he knew it was a lie. He'd only caught a glimpse of the thing they'd hit, but a little itch at the back of his brain told him that it had *not* been a deer. He just hoped it wasn't some wayward dog or...or...

JD was suddenly fourteen again, tearing down country roads in his father's car, pulling donuts at the graveled inter-sections. As he crested the hill next to Holke's farms, he spied the family of raccoons crossing the road a second too late. The thump-thump of little bodies hitting the undercarriage froze his blood. All he wanted was a little joyride while his pop slept one off, and now he was guilty of raccoonicide.

"You just going to stand there pulling your pud or are you going help us?"

The voice startled JD out of his reverie, and he looked around for its source. He found it in the person of a fiery redhead standing beside the now-damaged Honda. And if looks could kill…

JD blinked. The woman was decked out in a girlified version of a Huck Finn outfit—cutoff shorts, suspenders, checkered shirt tied in front, exposing her midriff. JD grinned. Girl trumps guilt every time.

"Howdy!" he called.

"Fuck your howdy," came a second voice. Battling tangled brush, a second, similarly-dressed—or similarly *undressed*— woman extracted herself from the passenger's side. She had a shock of blonde hair and muscles to spare.

The woman headed straight for him. She made a striking impression—the ripped physique of a weightlifter and the skimpy outfit of a stripper. The sheer force of her coming *toward* him caused JD to take a step back.

JD gulped. He needed backup. These women looked like they wanted to tear him apart, and he hadn't even been driving!

He held up a trembling finger, urging them to wait as he retreated to the truck.

"Rowdy! Get out here," he called.

"How bad is it?" Rowdy grimaced. "Did I kill it?"

"Huh?" For a moment, JD didn't have a clue as to what Rowdy was talking about. But then…

Oh, yeah…we hit something.

That could wait.

"There are some gals out here who *really* wanna talk to you."

Rowdy snapped out of his stupor. "Gals? What gals?"

JD urged Rowdy out of the truck and pointed him toward the women stewing next to their wrecked car.

"Holy Mark Twain," Rowdy said under his breath.

The women wore matching outfits, looking for all the world like some kind of novelty act. JD had to work hard not to gawk. They were a different kind of fine.

The blonde was busy taking photos of the damage with her phone while the redhead poked about under the hood, assessing the damage to the steaming vehicle.

"I hope you boys have your insurance paid up," the blonde said, angrily snapping pics. "This is going to cost you." *Snap.* "This is going to cost you big time." *Snap, snap.*

The redhead slammed the hood closed. "Looks like we blew a rod."

"Lucky rod," Rowdy said, probably louder than he meant to.

"Are you kidding me?" the blonde said. "We're standing right here, dude."

Thrown off, Rowdy blurted, "I'm Rowdy."

Jesus, Rowdy.

JD had seen this before. His friend spoke a good game, but when confronted with a real live, flesh and blood woman, he became a quivering mass—a condition obviously exacerbated by the shock of the accident.

The blonde turned in disbelief. "I don't care if you're the Queen of Jolly Fuckin' England; you just royally screwed up my night!"

"Look," JD said, glancing down at the name embroidered next to the woman's cleavage, "Honey, is it? Honey, I think we can all agree this was an accident, pure and simple."

"An accident?" He had her attention.

"Yeah. See, my buddy and I were just out for a spin when some critter jumped in our path. I'm no lawyer, but I'm pretty sure that falls under the "Act of God" umbrella where accidents are concerned."

Honey laughed. "Wait, you're *not* a lawyer? Shit, you could've fooled me. State Farm is going have a field day with you." She wrinkled her nose. "Nice ear."

JD's hand went to his ear before he could tell it not to—it was hot and wet with blood. The jolt of the collision must have coaxed Kate's buckshot wound back to life. He could feel the pellets lodged within.

"Just a goodbye kiss from my ex."

"JD?"

It was the redheaded driver who spoke, and JD suddenly realized that, despite her sexy Tom Sawyer get-up, she looked awfully familiar. Something about her eyes...no, her tone of voice...no...

The name on the woman's chest was Ruby, and the look on her face told him that wherever they had met, he probably hadn't been on his best behavior.

"You know this guy, Ruby?" Honey asked.

"Unfortunately, yes."

JD grinned dumbly and snapped his fingers, trying to jog his memory. "Oh, hey! I thought I recognized you. You're... uh...we met over at...uh...where'd we meet again?"

"Forget it." Ruby grabbed her phone. "Honey, I'm going to text Chester and let him know we need a tow."

"He's not going to be happy," Honey warned.

"When is he ever?"

Rowdy, who had been staring at the women like a fool staring at the sun, finally spoke up.

"Why are you dressed like that?"

"Because we like it, that's why," Honey said, whirling on him. "We *love* wearing skimpy little outfits so guys like you can ogle us and try to get in our pants. It's what we fuckin' *live* for."

"Oh...'cause you kinda look like them Huckleberry Girls from the beer posters."

"We *are* the Huckleberry Girls, you dipshit. Although we'll probably get fired now since you assholes are going to make us miss our gig."

"Chester's not picking up," Ruby said, slipping her phone into her purse.

"Where's your gig?" JD asked.

"Some shithole called The Dock," Honey said. "We've been trying to find it for the last hour. It's not showing up on my phone, and Chester's directions are crap."

"You mean Doc's Dockside?" JD asked, perking up. "We were just heading there ourselves, weren't we, Rowdy?"

"Well, we were thinking about it."

Damn it, Rowdy!

"Why don't we give you a lift?" JD offered.

"Pickup only seats three," Rowdy said, shaking his head.

Damn it, Rowdy!

"We could squish," JD offered.

"You wish," Honey said.

"See?" Rowdy said, hands raised. "It's not gonna work."

"Damn it, Rowdy!" JD said, this time aloud. "We ran

these pretty ladies off the road; the least we can do is give them a ride to their gig and call in a tow." Before Rowdy could counter, JD added, "I'll sit in the back."

"I don't care how I get there as long as I get there," Honey said, clapping her hands. "Mama needs those tips."

"I don't know," Ruby said, eyeballing JD.

"Come on, Ruby," Honey said. "My root canal isn't going to pay for itself. Pop the back."

"Fine." Ruby grabbed a hefty duffel bag from the car and slammed the door.

Rowdy pulled JD aside.

"I thought it was just gonna be you and me."

"It was. And now, it's not."

Rowdy yawned nervously as the women converged on the open hatch, extracting a couple of large equipment bags.

JD clapped his friend on the back.

"They're pretty gals, huh?"

"Yup."

"Don't be so jittery."

"I'm not."

"Then stop fiddling with your belt buckle."

Rowdy stuck his hands in his pockets.

Honey turned to them, a bag in her arms. "Please, don't offer to help."

"Okay," Rowdy said.

"I'll take it!" JD pushed past Rowdy and grabbed Honey's load. It was as heavy as a sandbag.

Damn, those arms of hers are solid steel.

Ruby appeared with her bag.

"You're the porter? Fine."

She stacked her duffle on top of Honey's, and JD felt his

knees yelp under the weight. Did Ruby actually smile at his discomfort? JD stumbled over to the pickup with his load, every protruding rock in the road threatening to sprain his ankle.

Where the hell did he know her from? Because the gal sure as heck seemed to know him. Some late-night tequila binge at Mud Daubers? The county fair? Community service? Where?

He dropped the bags into the payload. No worries. He'd get to the bottom of it soon enough.

"All right," he said, turning back to the group. "Let's get this show on the road!"

But Rowdy, Ruby, and Honey took no notice of him. Their collective focus was directed somewhere else entirely.

The Airstream.

He took a step toward them, but Rowdy held up a warning hand.

"What's the deal?"

A miserable, guttural howl rose, and JD froze.

Oh, yeah...

The impact.

The hair.

The blood.

...we hit something.

And now that *something* was crawling out from underneath the camper.

SIX

A small, twisted figure stared up at JD. Its limbs bent in all the wrong directions. It sported a wild mess of hair and a scraggly beard that hung off its face as if badly glued there.

It was also *way* too small to be a man.

Oh, God! JD thought. *We hit a kid.*

He reluctantly bent down to get a better look. This was so much worse than the raccoons.

Its painted eyes were the first giveaway. That and the fact that the thing looked suspiciously like...

Jesus?

JD laughed, relieved. "It's just a doll!"

A doll it was, or rather a ventriloquist dummy, like the kind that comedian Jeff Dunham used in his act. The dummy's jaw hung slack as if, in the last moment before the impact, it realized how well and truly fucked it was.

The strange thing was it was moving. Seemingly of its own accord.

The dummy clapped its ruined jaw.

40

Clap-clap!

JD bolted upright.

"Screw me sideways..." Honey whispered.

The mini-Jesus emerged from its hiding place, and it wasn't alone. A tangled mess of a man dragged himself forward. He had the look and stink of roadkill, which, it was dawning on JD, he actually was. The man pulled himself along on his belly with one hand, his other seemingly entangled in the doll's innards.

Clap-clap!

The dummy lunged forward as if warning the group of the horror bringing up the rear.

At first, JD's brain couldn't process what he was seeing. His eyes told him it was a man. But men had faces, didn't they? The thing emerging from beneath the Airstream did not.

The crawling horror's head was nothing but pulp, and JD's mind flitted back to the grill of Rowdy's truck—the glistening gristle embedded within.

"You said we hit a deer!" Rowdy cried.

"I thought we did!" JD replied.

"Does that look like a deer to you?"

"I don't know what the fuck that is!"

The monstrosity belched blood. JD had to admit to himself that he'd been wrong. They hadn't hit something— they had hit *someone.*

Clap-clap!

The man stumbled to his feet, free hand grasping for the foursome, the other working the dummy like a Muppet from hell. From the look of his tattered uniform, the man was the world's oldest boy scout. He tried to scream but, with no face, no mouth, no vocal cords, all he could manage was a sound somewhere between a howl and a wet fart.

Rowdy unsheathed his Bowie knife. "Get behind me, girls."

"Who the hell are you calling a girl?" Honey spat, promptly picking up a rock and hurling it at the thing's ragged head. The stone struck just below where the man's left ear used to be, tearing a gash in its flesh.

The creature—for it really couldn't rightly be called a man anymore—stopped short and bent its shattered head. Vertebrae snapped like popcorn.

JD's eyes went wide as teeth sprouted from the wound. They punched through muscle and tendon, not giving a shit about the damage they caused. They emerged shiny white and in incredible numbers. The teeth jostled about in the raw flesh until they formed a new orifice, the circle of incisors reminding JD of a blooming onion.

Honey picked up another rock.

"What do you think you're doin'?" Rowdy cried. "Don't you think that damn thing's got enough teeth?"

"I don't see you doing anything," Honey said.

Rowdy shifted his knife from one hand to the other. "I'm weighin' the situation."

"Just like a man," Honey scoffed, rearing back to throw. "Got something in your hand but you don't know what to do with it."

She let fly with the second rock. This one struck the dummy in the jaw, knocking it clean off. Now it more resembled the man holding it.

The mangled mess that had once been Pastor Jim bellowed at the starry sky, and in the distance, his cries were answered. Whooping, hungry howls filled the night, sending a chill straight down to JD's tailbone.

"Shit." JD wasn't much of a hunter. His grandfather Ti had once called him 'the lousiest shot west of Hell.' But even though his shooting average stood at one hit to thirty-five misses where deer were concerned, he had brought one important skill to the table, and that was his uncanny ability to locate prey. He might suck at nailing a target, but his inner compass and keen ear made him a better-than-average tracker.

But now his gift was failing him. He couldn't for the life of him pinpoint the location of the howls in the woods.

"Folks," he said, "I'm gonna suggest we get the hell outta here." JD nudged Rowdy to get him moving. Startled, his friend promptly dropped his knife. It clattered to the ground.

"Dammit!" Rowdy cussed, retrieving the knife from the dirt.

"Unbelievable," Honey snorted.

Out in the woods, branches snapped as something crashed through the brush. *Many* somethings. The shambling abomination that was once a scoutmaster turned at the sound.

JD puzzled over this. *How the hell can it hear when it ain't got no ears?*

The spray of teeth protruding from the man's neck quivered with each approaching footfall.

It's listening with its goddamned teeth...

The ex-scoutmaster loosed a terrible holler, releasing a spray of bloody spittle from its open throat, painting the air red. High-pitched shrieks replied as the first of the horde clambered into view.

There was no mistaking it this time—the figure that emerged from the darkness was a child. A child in a viscera-drenched scout uniform. A miniature copy of the creature holding the jawless Jesus.

The scout stumbled onto the road, sniffing the air, mouth open wide, a satellite dish searching for a signal.

Rowdy obliged.

"Mother humper..." he whispered.

The bloody boy spun in their direction.

"Way to go, Rowdy," JD said as the scout rushed them. He grabbed up a fallen branch and snapped it in two, fashioning a makeshift club. If skinny dipping in a public fountain had earned him a night in the slammer, he could only imagine how long Cal the Cop would incarcerate him for doing what he'd have to do now. And that was to knock this little sucker's head off.

"Behind you!" Ruby cried.

JD whirled about, and his stomach sank. There was a reason he hadn't been able to pinpoint the direction of the creatures' advance—they were approaching from all sides.

Two more scouts exited the woods. One bent unnaturally at the waist, its spine snapped in two. Its limp torso hung to the side, its legs working overtime to maintain balance. What the second scout lacked in arms, it made up for with mouths. Raw, red orifices sprouted from each shoulder, snapping hungrily as if ready to chow down in Dolby stereo.

"Watch it!" This time it was Honey giving the heads up. More savage munchkins tumbled out of the woods, some pulling themselves across the gravel road, others staggering into the clearing on broken legs.

The branch grew instantly heavy in JD's hands. The

toothy troop had gotten the jump on them. They were surrounded.

"How about that ride?" Ruby was at JD's elbow.

"Rowdy?" JD said, inching toward the truck. "Shall we scram?"

Rowdy stood mesmerized by the sight of the swaying, squealing scoutmaster.

"Rowdy?"

His friend blinked. "Scram? Yeah...good idea."

"Cut the chatter." Honey hauled off and beaned a sucker-boy with a forceful underhand toss, catching it in the teeth with a sickening crunch. "I got shotgun."

Honey grabbed Ruby by the arm and launched her toward the pickup. The two women were halfway to the truck before JD knew what had happened.

"Gimme your keys." JD stuck out his hand.

"What makes you think you're driving?"

JD glanced at the Bowie knife shaking in Rowdy's hand like he was conducting "Flight of the Bumblebee."

"What makes you think *you* are?"

"Fair point."

The faceless scoutmaster took a step toward them, and as he did so, his chest split open, buttons popping from his uniform. The creature's guts spilled out of its chest cavity as if something were trying to burrow its way out.

What's it up to now?

JD didn't wait around to find out.

"Ready?"

"Not in the fucking slightest," Rowdy said.

"On three. One..."

JD took aim with the branch.

"Two..."

He flung it javelin-style toward the thing. Its point struck home, piercing a protruding, purple lung, which burped with all the force of a punctured tire.

"Three!"

JD took off after the Huckleberries.

A particularly grabby scout with a strobing headlamp popped out between the camper and the pickup. JD spun, executing a move he'd perfected escaping Walmart security. He slammed into the tailgate, rounded the back of the pickup, and climbed into the cabin where Ruby and Honey anxiously awaited him.

"Go!" Honey shouted.

"We gotta wait for Rowdy."

Ruby placed a hand on his shoulder. Her touch was like live current.

"We have to go, JD."

"He can make it!"

"Look..."

JD turned his head. He caught the sucker-scouts converging. And at the center of their circle stood Rowdy, knife upraised. The circle closed on his friend.

Rowdy...why didn't you run?

"He's done for!" Honey shouted. "Get it in gear!"

The woman threw the pickup into drive. JD fought for control of the shift, but Honey was as strong as a WWF wrestler.

"I'm not dying today," Honey snarled, trying to snake her leg over Ruby to press on the gas. "I still have too much shit to do."

"So does Rowdy!"

The pickup bounced as something tumbled into the truck bed.

Maybe I should've listened to her.

"Haul ass!" a ragged voice called from behind them.

JD whipped around. Plunked down in the back of the pickup was Rowdy.

"Good to have you back, buddy!"

"I said git, Speers!"

JD threw the truck in gear and stamped on the gas. The pickup-camper combo shuddered, and then lurched to life. Frustrated screams followed them as they sped off down the road.

"I told you he'd make it," JD said, throwing Honey some major side-eye.

"Just drive, will you?" Honey spat.

Oh, I'll drive, JD thought. *And if one of those little fuckers dares to cross my path, I'll splatter it across the road.*

SEVEN

"Hey! Numbnuts!" Honey cried. "Watch the road."

A pothole the size of Texas loomed up in the headlights. JD swerved, just catching the edge of it—the Airstream's right wheels hit the hole dead on, causing it to bounce dangerously, threatening to yank loose.

"Jesus, Ruby, this guy's going to get us killed."

"Back off, will you?" Ruby said.

"Sorry if I want to make it through this day in one piece."

"We all do, Honey."

"Well, his driving sure casts doubt on that assumption."

JD didn't say a word. He hoped that by not engaging, the woman would lose steam and fizzle out.

"What's the plan?" Ruby asked.

"Heading to Doc's," JD replied. Short and sweet.

"The bar?" Ruby shook her head. "I really think we should go to the police."

Oh, yeah. Cal and his buddies would just love *to have me serve myself up on a platter.*

"There's nothing but woods between us and the police

station. We don't know how many of those things are out there. We gotta get somewhere safe. Doc's is only another mile or so," he said. "And I don't know about you, but I could sure use a stiff drink." He called back through the busted rear window to Rowdy. "That sound good to you? A stiff drink?"

"Yeah, yeah..." Rowdy growled. "Just get there pronto."

"Hey, you okay?"

"Yeah, I'm okay. Why you askin' me if I'm okay? Jesus, just drive!"

"Alright, alright!" JD was getting it from all sides.

He caught Ruby staring at him...no, examining him. Where the hell did he know her from? The uptilt of her nose, the curve of her frown—all *so* familiar, and yet...

The woods were becoming patchier the farther they drove. They passed a couple of cabins that the elements had reduced to little more than kindling. Moss had taken possession of the structures, seemingly intent on consuming them. But that was nature, wasn't it? Eat or get eaten.

"What the hell were those things?" JD asked, not expecting an answer from anyone. How could there be any coherent answer to what they had all just witnessed?

"Monsters." Honey's blunt response hung in the air, daring anyone to challenge it. "How they got that way... rabies, swamp fever, whatever...who knows? But...yeah, monsters. The fucking things were monsters."

That put a damper on all conversation. JD drove on. A glow appeared over the tops of the trees. They were getting closer to the river, closer to Doc's. What happened when they got there was anyone's guess. Someone would call the cops, that much was certain. He was surprised one of the women sitting next to him hadn't done so already, but then he realized neither of them appeared to have their phones on them. Unless they had them squirreled away somewhere in those tight cutoff shorts.

The cops would come, he'd be shoved in the back of a cruiser, and that would be that. Grand theft Airstream.

He'd have to vamoose as soon as they reached Doc's, take off, and never look back. He couldn't do hard time. Hell, he'd hardly managed soft time. Let the others call the cops and field their questions—he had to get while the getting was good.

The woods flanking the road thinned, and the bar appeared up ahead. Doc's Dockside Tavern: a metal-roofed dive hugging the banks of the Mississippi. Even at this distance, the beat of a country classic could be heard. It was a country boy's wet dream.

A large, red neon sign buzzed atop the roof, the occasional letter flickering in and out. Doc had paid top dollar for the sign a couple years back, but after a couple of weeks, it began having electrical fits. Now it looked like a glorified bug zapper.

"What a shithole," Honey said. "Leave it to Chester to sniff out the worst of the worst."

"A shithole beats being out in the open with those things," Ruby countered.

A smattering of cars and trucks sat parked out front, and a jon boat bobbed in the water, tethered to an aluminum dock. Not exactly a packed house, but still enough folks to make JD nervous.

Park. Say your goodbyes and book it, he thought.

He had just hit the grass-covered parking lot when something landed on the cabin roof with a whomp. JD and his passengers screamed in unison.

Dots of blood hit the windshield. JD instinctively flipped on the wipers, managing only to turn the dots into a smear.

A wide, fleshy circle suddenly slapped against the windshield, attaching itself like an octopus sucker. Little teeth clicked against the glass. It was a goddamn mouth.

JD pressed the wiper switch, and a spray of blue fluid hit the windshield, washing away the smeared blood, revealing two animal eyes set into a child's face. The scout was hanging upside down, a sash filled with merit badges tangling with the wiper blades. He gnawed at the glass like a lamprey trying to feed.

"Where'd *that* come from?" Ruby cried.

"Damn it!" Rowdy piped up behind them. "Musta been hiding on top of the camper. Watch yourselves!"

JD peered past the slobbering sucker and spied a pristine Toyota Ram parked at the back of the joint. Its plate read: *HKL-BRY.*

He lined it up in his sights.

"What do you think you're doing?" Honey yelled.

"Buckle up," JD said to Ruby. "Hold tight, Rowdy!"

"Hold tight?"

Sharp teeth pierced the glass as the thing on the roof bit through the windshield.

Putting the Ram in his sights, JD channeled his inner Luke Skywalker. *Almost there...*

"What do you mean, *hold tight?*"

JD hit the gas.

Whunk!

The front of the pickup plowed into the Ram's tailgate.

The brand spanking new vehicle was much more fortified than the hunk of junk Rowdy drove, and so the old pickup's hood crumpled instantly. JD hadn't had a lot of runway to pick up speed, but they were still going a good thirty-five miles an hour when they collided.

The impact tossed JD forward, seatbelt biting deep. Rowdy let out a shout as he tumbled across the truck bed. The collision dislodged the sucker, sending the scout hurtling field goal-style into the back of the Ram. JD thought he detected shattering glass as the boy hit.

The passenger side airbag didn't so much deploy as mount an ineffectual escape. JD's airbag was content to remain inside the steering wheel. He shouldn't have expected anything less from Rowdy's clunker.

"Everybody okay?"

Honey reached across Ruby and slugged him in the arm. The awkward angle should have made for a less effective punch, but the woman still dealt him a painful blow.

"Ah, God! You're welcome," he snarled.

Honey threw off her belt and opened her door. "It's been a slice, asshole. Come on, Ruby." And she was gone, out of the pickup and running for the bar's rear entrance.

"Your friend's a real piece of work," JD said.

"Let's go before that thing is back on its feet," Ruby urged.

"I...I wasn't planning on going in." The last thing JD needed was more witnesses.

"You just going to take off?"

"No, I..."

Ruby scowled at him. "You haven't changed one bit, have you?"

She turned and slid out of the truck, leaving JD to wonder yet again who the hell she was.

But there was no time to waste. Once the women hit the bar and started telling their side of the story, it would be too late for a clean getaway.

JD threw the pickup in reverse.

Gears ground like a giant's teeth. Steam shot out from under the crumpled hood. Every warning signal lit up on the dashboard.

Not good.

As if activated by the alarms, the scout in the Ram's truck bed jumped up and let loose a pained howl that set JD's teeth on edge.

Not good at all.

"Gimme a chance to get out, will ya?" Rowdy roared.

"Little busy right now, Rowdy!"

He tried throwing the truck into drive, into reverse, back to drive. Nothing worked, and he had to accept the inevitable conclusion: it was time to abandon ship.

The sucker launched itself at the pickup, taking aim at the hole in the windshield it had already started. Picking up where it left off, it gnawed at the glass, gums bleeding. A few more bites and they'd be face-to-face.

A ripping noise drew JD's attention to the steering wheel. The cover was unzipping itself, rubber splitting down the middle to reveal white fabric underneath.

Better late than never, JD thought, raising his arms in front of his face.

A second later, the airbag blew, filling the cabin, pressing JD back against the seat, and blocking the beastie's ghastly, gnashing jaws.

The sucker was undeterred by the sudden appearance of the inflated bag, choosing to continue doing what it did best —bite.

While the creature went to town on the airbag, JD squirmed out the door and flopped to the ground. He somersaulted to a standing position and turned back quickly to the pickup. The sucker was busy rending the airbag into shreds.

Ditching the Dockside was no longer an option. Besides, JD couldn't leave his favorite bar unprepared for what was coming.

Time to hoof it.

"Come on, Rowdy!"

"Just a sec."

"Let's go!"

"Jesus, I'm right behind you. Go!"

The tangle of trucks barred his path to the back entrance —the way the Huckleberries had disappeared—so it was the front entrance for him. JD bolted for the door.

He dodged a Turquoise VW Beetle, slammed his knee into a motorcycle, vaulted over a metal trough of cigarette butts, and hit the front door without slowing.

Bright lights, blaring music, and the scent of sour beer and sawdust greeted JD as he stumbled into the bar. All eyes turned his way.

"We gotta lock this place down. Now!"

EIGHT

The moment the words were out of JD's mouth he realized he was in trouble. Instead of leaping to their feet in response to his rallying cry, the dozen or so beer-guzzling regulars offered up nothing but blank stares.

I'm competing with a goddamn jukebox.

JD strode over to the corner where the jukebox sat next to a pile of lumber, awaiting the day it could become a raised stage. He was startled to find Ruby standing next to the jukebox—a life-size cutout of her, that is. She winked at him in all her cardboard glory, above her the words, *Be a man! Suck it up. Huckleberry Beer.* A metal trough filled high with ice and said beer sat nearby.

He leaned over and yanked the jukebox's plug free. The speakers about the place crackled and went silent. The Saturday night crowd booed, tossing bar nuts at him. Undeterred, he tried again.

"We have to lock this place down!"

A German Shepherd popped up from behind the bar,

paws on the bar top. The dog growled, unhappy with JD's tone.

"Easy, Dubya," the bar owner said. He regarded JD. "If you don't like Hank, you could've just said so."

What the...? It took JD a moment to realize the song he'd just interrupted was "I'll Never Get Out Of This World Alive" by that ol' hillbilly Shakespeare himself, Hank Williams.

At least the man in the Hawaiian shirt hadn't said what everyone was probably thinking—that he was off his nut. In fact, Doc Moser seemed pleasantly surprised to see him.

"Now, plug the tunes back in, and let's have a chat."

JD plugged in the jukebox, and Doc obliged by cranking the volume down a few notches. JD made a beeline for the bar, accidentally shoulder-checking Fisher, who was heading out for a smoke.

"Nice ear," Fisher said, eyeballing JD's bloody lobe. The wiry man in his trademark fishing vest was slow to anger, but if there was one person on earth who could push his buttons, it was JD Speers.

"I wouldn't go out there if I was you," JD warned.

"Never get between a man and his smoke," Fisher said, ignoring JD's advice and stepping outside.

Doc plonked a shot glass down in front of JD and pulled a bottle of the house whiskey from beneath the bar. "Have a shot, and stop bothering my customers."

This was *not* going how JD had expected. Where the hell were the Huckleberries? They'd made a run for it, but JD hadn't actually seen them make it inside. Maybe there were other suckers lying in wait for them. Maybe they were already dead. Or worse.

JD approached the bar warily. Dubya was still on high alert.

"Down, boy," Doc ordered. The dog complied with a grumble.

JD grabbed the shot and downed it. Doc's house liquors had always been the bottom of the barrel, and the whiskey he forced down was no exception. It tasted like battery acid mixed with wood tar. He sucked air through his teeth as the liquid burned its way south.

JD slammed the shot glass down on the bar, and Doc refilled it.

"So, what's got your panties in a bunch?" Doc asked.

JD considered pounding the second shot but decided he needed to get the words out before the rut gut went to his head. Doc eyed him quizzically. A veterinarian in his previous life, Doc was adept at diagnosing others' behavior, be they man or malamute. He wrinkled his brow, bringing his massive eyebrows together to form a concerned V. Best not to keep him in suspense.

"Outside. Little monsters. They're coming. They bite. Little monsters. We gotta lock down." He spat out the words like an avid cocaine user. This having been accomplished, he gulped down the shot—it burned even more than the first.

Doc smiled at him and returned the bottle to its hiding place.

"Alright, you got me. Thought you had real news. Little monsters?" Doc chuckled. "You pay for your next shot."

"You gotta listen to me!"

JD reached across the bar and grabbed Doc by his shirt, and as he did so, he remembered two things: one, that although Doc looked like Santa Claus, he didn't take kindly to being touched; and two, being as he had spent most of his adult life studying muscles, bones, and the nervous system, Doc knew a lot about pain.

The older man caught JD's hand in his and, applying pressure with just two fingers, twisted ever so slightly. The hurt Doc caused was so intense that JD's legs buckled.

"Now," Doc said, still grinning, "you wanna start over?"

JD slapped the bar like a wrestler tapping out. Doc released his grip—the pain abated.

JD tried a different tack. "I came here with two women. Wearing sexy costumes. Did they make it inside?"

"He must mean the beer gals," a young woman said, turning away from the sink where she'd been cleaning a mountain of glassware. As always, Weena looked frazzled—some folks thrived on the chaos of working a dive bar, some did not. Weena was one of the latter. "Their boss is in the back waiting for them, but I haven't seen them yet. Hon? You see the beer gals?"

A baby-faced kid in a camo coat looked up from his potato wedges. "Only in my dreams."

"Seriously, Bo?"

Bo smirked. "You're the only beer gal I got eyes for."

Weena whapped him with her bar rag.

Doc nodded his head. "You? Hanging out with the Huckleberry Beer Girls? Color me impressed, Speers."

JD was getting nowhere fast. Who knew when that little sucker might come crashing through the door, teeth bared and ready to rumble? How long before his friends caught wind of the barfly buffet over at Doc's? And where the hell was Rowdy?

JD snatched the beer bottle from the fellow straddling

the stool to his right. He'd seen the guy in here a few times before but didn't know his name. Buck? Chuck? It didn't matter. The only thing that mattered was getting everyone's attention.

He raised the bottle and dashed it to the floor. Glass and suds exploded across the faded linoleum. Dubya leaped back up, barking his head off.

"Listen up!" He ignored the curses that rose from the crowd. "We're all dead if you don't *listen up!*"

"No, you listen up, Speers."

JD whirled about at the sound of the voice, and his mouth went dry.

Woof. Woof was coming for him.

Gareth Wolf was Doc's go-to bouncer on weekends. Doc threw the guy a few bucks to keep the Dockside in order. One look at the Brothers of Boden patch on his leather made any potential troublemaker think twice. Nicknamed 'Woof' for the way locals pronounce his family name, the mountain of a man didn't take shit from anyone, even regulars.

He moved up fast on JD, and patrons parted in his path— the overheads glinting off his bald head, his hearing aids buzzing like angry bees. His bulging biceps, developed during years as a roadie, twitched in anticipation of the altercation to come.

"We got a problem?" The man's words came out nasal and mushy, no doubt the result of his hearing loss and mashed nose. This was *not* the sort of attention JD had been looking for.

"Look, Woof, lemme explain—"

The leather-clad giant took a step closer, and JD found himself staring up the man's flared nostrils.

"How 'bout you don't? Take a hike."

"I know you don't like me."

The big man sighed. "This ain't about me, Speers."

"But I'm trying to explain—"

"Explain faster."

JD risked placing a hand on the man's massive arm. He had to break through to Woof, even if it meant getting his own arm broken in the process.

"This is gonna sound crazy, Woof, but—"

The room erupted with the sound of bluegrass music—a cacophony of banjos and mandolins.

"Ladies and gentlemen of Doc's Dockside Tavern...are you ready for this?" a disembodied male voice said, doing battle with the music. "I'm proud to present the one, the only..."

Whoops of anticipation rose from the men in the tavern and not a few women.

"The Huckleberry Girls!"

The bluegrass music morphed into bone-rattling heavy metal. A cloud of stage fog poured out from the back hallway. A pitiful smattering of lasers pierced the rolling mist.

And then...nothing.

The speaker mumbled at someone off-mic before redoubling his efforts.

"You want 'em? You got 'em! The Huckleberries!"

The bass beat pounded, and the mist rolled on in, but the Huckleberries were nowhere to be seen.

"Goddamn it," whispered the man with the microphone. "What's the matter with you? Get your butts out there."

An audible struggle ensued as someone attempted to wrestle the mic from the announcer's hands. It reminded JD of the old-time radio plays his father used to listen to while destroying yet another case of Old Milwaukee.

The patrons looked around in confusion. Was this part of the show?

The man with the mic squealed. JD recognized the sound of someone getting bitten. Rapid breathing sounded from the speakers. Then someone spoke.

"We've got to get out of here! They're coming! They're coming!"

It was Ruby.

JD took a couple of running steps into the fog when the front door creaked open so hard its hinges cracked.

A figure stumbled into the bar and heaved a big sigh of relief—Rowdy, at last.

JD's friend was spattered with blood from head to foot. And he had something meaty attached to his belt.

Sweet Jesus...was that a head?

"Aw, fuck it," Rowdy bellowed. "I'm gonna need a little help."

NINE

Rowdy flicked his Bowie knife, splattering blood across the linoleum floor. The flesh ball at his waist groaned, and Rowdy winced. He gave the thing a few frantic stabs with his knife, but the thing held firm.

"What the hell is that?" Woof's attention had shifted from JD to Rowdy, giving JD the opportunity to duck away from the bouncer.

"What does it look like?" Rowdy spat. His voice rose in a mix of rage and fear. He gave the meat ball another stab for good measure. A muffled moan rose from his groin.

JD took a tentative step toward his friend.

"Them rabid rugrats don't give up easy. This here one latched on but good. I relieved it of its body, but I can't get it free."

"Damn, Rowdy."

Doc was out from behind the bar in a shot, Dubya trotting at his heels. The dog took one sniff in Rowdy's direction and snarled.

The old vet drew close to Rowdy but not *too* close. He

pulled a pair of readers from his shirt pocket and peered at the freakish protuberance at Rowdy's belt.

"Turn to the left," Doc whispered.

"You ain't gonna ask me to cough, are you, Doc?"

"Shut up and do it."

Rowdy turned. The bar let out a collective gasp as light fell on the face of the severed head clinging to Rowdy's belt buckle with its sharp teeth.

The head obviously belonged to one of the sucker-scouts JD and the crew had encountered back in the woods. Gone was any trace of innocent youth—the curly-haired kid had been transformed into a gnashing nightmare. All color had drained from its eyes and face, and its jaw worked overtime to remain attached to the American flag buckle at Rowdy's waist.

"Looks like your belt buckle saved your ass," Doc mused. "Or your Johnson, at least."

"God bless America," JD said.

Rowdy twitched as the head ground its teeth into his belt. "You gonna just stand there or are you gonna get this thing off me?"

JD looked to Doc—the man didn't seem all too eager to get any closer to the thing.

JD sighed. "Gimme your knife."

The blade was slick with blood, as was the handle. JD carefully extracted it from Rowdy's shaking hand, mindful not to drop it.

Ew...the blood is still warm.

As JD slipped the knife between the belt and Rowdy's jeans, the head's eyes flicked his way—dull eyes in bruised sockets watched his every move.

This is creepy as fuck.

JD began sawing away at the leather strap, and as he did so, the head hissed like an angry goose. The thing knew what he was up to and was pissed at the prospect of being cut loose.

"Don't stop!" Rowdy said.

JD redoubled his effort, arm pistoning up and down, cutting through the belt like it was the toughest steak on earth.

"Almost..." JD whispered. Just a few strokes more.

The head must have sensed it was about to lose the battle because before JD could make his final cuts, it released its hold on Rowdy's buckle and fell to the floor. It hit with a wet splat.

"Move!" Doc ordered.

Rowdy moved, leaping over the head and joining JD and Doc a safe distance away.

"Gimme my knife," Rowdy rumbled.

JD handed it over, steering clear of the severed head rocking back and forth on the floor.

"What are you going to do?" It was Weena, and like everyone else in the place, she looked to Doc to make the next move.

"How should I know?" Doc said. "I don't even know what I'm looking at."

"I'll take care of it," came a voice filled with drunken bravado. JD glanced over and spied the guy whose beer he'd snatched—Chuck? Buck?—slide off of his barstool.

"Stay where you are, Larry," Doc warned.

Larry? JD thought. *Great memory, Speers.*

The drunk harumphed and plopped back down on his stool, its metal legs making a wince-inducing *scree-ee*.

The head flipped over in response, landing on its face. It rose up on rows of teeth and scuttered about like a crab on a hotplate.

Everyone who had drawn close leaped back.

Its eyes rolled in its head as it gained its bearings. Its teeth worked in unison to propel it forward, like a millipede's legs, sharp points clicking across the linoleum.

A man burst into the room from the back hallway. He was a tall fellow, slim, decked out in a white jacket, blue jeans, and a mustache that pushed him over the line from good-looking to handsome. His arms were outstretched, and in each hand, he held a bottle of beer.

"Who's ready to get Hucked?"

"Read the room, Chester," Ruby said as she and Honey elbowed past the man. Crestfallen, the man took in the scene. The entire bar had its back to him.

JD was so fixated on Ruby's return that he didn't notice the head was scampering in his direction.

"Move!" the crowd shouted.

JD spied the danger just in time and leaped up onto a chair, teetering precariously.

"Thanks," he breathed.

Ruby pushed her way to the front of the crowd. She stared up at JD. "What are you doing up there?"

JD nodded at the head. Rudy's eyes went wide when she saw it. She gasped.

The head whirled about and gasped back.

This proved too much for Dubya—the dog let out a whimper and scurried back behind the bar.

"I told you there were monsters out there," JD said, hopping down from the chair. "Question is: what do we do with this fucking head?"

A disgruntled snort came from the back of the crowd, and Larry—not Buck or Chuck—shoved his way through.

"You pussies," Larry slurred. "I already told you I'd take care of it."

"No! Woof, stop him!"

But Doc's order came too late. Larry, perhaps overcome by some hazy memory of gridiron glories past, rushed the head and punted it toward the door.

JD had forgotten Fisher had stepped out for a cigarette. But when the man stepped back into the bar the very moment the sucker's head took flight, he remembered.

Never get between a man and his smoke.

The careening cranium struck Fisher square in the face.

Luckily for the old fellow, the head hit him neck first. Instead of a face full of barbed teeth, he got a mouthful of trachea. It dropped to the floor, leaving a trail of gore down Fisher's front.

"Outta the way!" Larry was going for the field goal. Before anyone could stop him, he drew back his leg and took his second shot.

This time, the teeth found purchase, biting through Larry's old work boot, eager for the flesh hiding inside. Larry let loose a bloodcurdling scream as teeth found toes.

"Get it off!" Larry's cries were pitiful, yet no one stepped up to the plate. If anything, the louder his pleas, the farther back everyone stepped.

"We gotta get it off him!" JD cried. He took a step toward Larry, ready to grab the head by the hair if necessary, but as he did so, teeth spiked from its severed neck, as if the head knew what he planned on doing and was having none of it.

Phalanges and metatarsals snapped. It was all just so horrible. But JD couldn't look away.

Something was happening to Larry's leg.

At first, JD thought it was a trick of the light—the goddamn lasers were still zipping around the room—but when Larry's pant leg began to burst at the seams, it was clear something was very, very wrong.

Larry's jeans split, revealing his pale thigh. Then, his thigh split, revealing teeth—bone-white, gnarled teeth, poking angrily through muscle and skin.

The poor drunk bastard wailed in agony as his leg morphed into a mouth. But the transformation didn't stop there—soon, he had new teeth sprouting from seemingly everywhere. His chest, the palms of his hands, his mouth. Each new tooth brought fresh waves of screaming pain.

And then, in a display that rivaled the greatest magic tricks ever performed, Larry split from crotch to crown.

JD's eyes went wide. One minute, Larry was whole; the next, he'd been halved. His ribcage opened up, his skull cracked up the middle, and his left and his right sides did battle for his internal organs. His last meal spilled forth for all to see—pepperoni pizza and breadsticks, from the look of it.

JD was beside himself. Unfortunately, so was Larry.

Everyone was too shocked to move.

Everyone but Woof.

The bouncer charged the split man, careful to avoid the patches of canines bursting through skin, and bum rushed both halves of him toward the door. The men hit the door with a wallop and tumbled together into the darkness beyond.

As the frightened crowd awaited the outcome of Woof's bold move, JD noticed Ruby was standing by his side. Her gaze, like everyone else's, was focus on the rectangle of black into which the drunk and the bouncer had disappeared.

"Glad you're safe," JD offered.

"Likewise," Ruby said, then tilted her head. "Although you better get that ear looked at."

She reached out and touched his ear. Either her fingers were ice cold or his ear was on fire.

He cleared his throat. "When I came in and didn't see you, I was afraid that—"

The fellow in the white jacket was suddenly at Ruby's side. "Everything okay here?"

"Yeah, Chester," Ruby said, closing her eyes. "Why wouldn't it be?"

"Let's get you away from the door."

Chester handed JD one of the beers in his hand, then took Ruby by the arm, and yanked her toward the bar.

The hair bristled on JD's neck. "Careful, buddy."

The man in the jacket didn't even reply. Trademark move of a trademark dick. JD hated him instantly.

He looked down at the bottle in his hand.

Huckleberry Beer – Real American Sour Made From Real American Huckleberries.

JD twisted the cap and took a sip.

Jesus, it tastes like vinegar.

Woof burst through the door. His leather was ripped, his face scratched, but he seemed otherwise unharmed.

But, damn...the man was trembling.

A dissonant chorus of howls echoed from the parking lot. Hell was on its way to the Dockside.

JD dropped his beer, Real American Sour splattering across the floor.

"I'm with Speers," Woof said, panic rising in his voice. "We need to lock this place down."

TEN

The crowd made quick work of it. Tables and chairs became barricades. Patrons salvaged the half-finished stage in the corner for wood and tools. Screw guns and hammers did their work, and in a matter of minutes, Doc's Dockside was battened down tight.

A second after JD drove his last screw into a plank blocking the window near the jukebox, he heard the scraping sound of fingers on wood.

The suckers had found them.

The bar was abuzz with frantic chatter. Doc put a stop to that.

"Hush up, all of you." Doc had a voice so authoritative it could make a drill sergeant jump. He stepped in front of the main door—now covered with half a dozen two-by-fours and some metal signs ripped from the walls—and held up his hands like a preacher addressing his congregation. "We've got a situation here, but let's not lose our heads. How many of you bastards ignored my sign?"

Doc stuck his thumb at a hand-painted plaque hanging over the bar that read, *No Guns Please—Graveyard is Full.*

Half the men in the place sheepishly raised their hands.

"Good to know we've got some armed illiterates in the house," Doc said. "Has anyone called 911?"

JD and the rest of the crowd stared blankly. 911? What the hell was 911?

One screen lit up, then another as folks fumbled at their phones. Soon everyone in Doc's was calling the authorities.

JD abstained.

He glanced over at Rowdy, who was at the bar helping himself to a top-shelf tequila shot. He approached his friend, hands up.

"If I'd have known you were tangling with one of those things out there in the parking lot," JD said, "I would've hung back and helped out."

Rowdy glared at him, and for a moment, JD thought the man might strike him over the head with the Reposado. Then, he handed JD the bottle.

JD took a swig of tequila. It went down smooth.

Damn, this is how the other half lives.

"How'd you...? You know...?" JD said, drawing a line across his neck with the bottle's mouth.

Rowdy grabbed back the booze.

"Sheer force of will, my friend. I told myself, 'Rowdy, ain't no chance in hell you're gonna be taken down by a kindy-gartner.' So, I did what I had to do."

"Cut a kid's head off."

"Damn straight," Rowdy said, downing a little extra liquid courage to steady himself.

The two men passed the bottle back and forth, surveying

the scene. Small groups were forming as patrons relayed the results of their phone calls to each other.

"What do you think the cops are gonna think about this?" Rowdy asked.

JD took a double swig. "All I know is that when they get here, I'm up shit's creek."

"I'd say that's a distinct possibility."

Amidst the flurry of conversation, two people stood out. Chester, the beer douche, had Ruby cornered and was speaking low to her. Whatever he was saying had the effect of causing her shoulders to slump.

"Ever figure out how you know her?" Rowdy asked.

"Who?"

"That strawberry blonde over yonder."

JD's mind spun but came up goose eggs. "Haven't a clue."

"Listen up!" This time it was Woof grabbing everyone's attention. "We've got cops on the way. In the meantime, I'm heading up to the roof to see what's what. Anybody want to come with?"

JD raised his hand. "Me. I do."

"Well, come along," Woof said, heading for the back.

"You coming?" JD asked, looking to Rowdy.

"I got no interest whatsoever."

"Okay, then."

In the end, only Woof, Fisher, and JD chose to suss out the situation from above. The bouncer led the others to kitchen where Luis, the Dockside's lone cook, had been hiding out. Woof led the others up a steel ladder attached to the wall and through a small hatch in the ceiling. Luis looked on, content to remain in his little domain.

The sky was overcast, clouds hiding the stars. There was

no moon that night, which made it all the more difficult to maneuver safely atop the slick metal.

JD pulled his phone and ignited its flashlight.

"Get that out of my eyes," Woof snarled.

"Sorry."

"How many of those things are out here, you think?" Fisher asked, boot heels pressed down hard to hold his position.

"We ran into maybe half a dozen on the back road," JD said. "They were little, but they packed a wallop."

"What'd you think they are?" Fisher pressed.

"Bad news," was all JD could think of to say.

Woof pulled a tactical flashlight and trained it on the parking lot below, catching each vehicle in the beam of light.

He landed on the Airstream and the wounded pickups. The damage to Rowdy's truck was even worse than JD could have imagined.

"That your handiwork?" Woof asked.

"Afraid so."

Woof shook his head. "That Chester fellow ain't gonna be too happy with you."

"Why? That's not his Ram, is it?"

Woof didn't say a word.

"Is it?"

"Look there!" Fisher was pointing toward the bright circle cast by Woof's flashlight.

JD looked down. There, caught in the beam, was a figure swaying next to Fisher's Oldsmobile. It raised its head, long teeth catching the light.

"Doesn't look so little to me," Fisher said.

The man was right. The sucker in the spotlight was *not*

one of the scouts, although it did sport a uniform. But instead of shorts, this newcomer wore slacks and a khaki shirt.

"That's Al Garner," Woof said. "Works for the forest service. Guess they got him too."

Sucker Al hissed, perhaps sensing the men watching him from the roof. Another figure stumbled into view—a young woman in flannel.

"And that's Jenny from the Gas-2-Go," Fisher said, gawking at the unnatural way her head lay on her right shoulder. "Where'd you say you first ran into these things?"

"A mile and a half up County 3," JD said.

"It's spreading." Woof spat over the edge. "Gas-2-Go's a mile in the other direction."

"If it's spreading, why are they all coming here?" Fisher asked.

"How do you lure fish?" JD asked in turn.

"Bait."

"We're the bait."

"Shit!" JD and Fisher jumped at Woof's outburst.

"What the hell, dude?" Fisher complained.

"We got more incoming."

Woof scanned the lot with his flashlight. Al Garner and Jenny had company—lots of company.

A pair of women tangled in the remains of a nylon tent crawled out from the trees. And just joining the crowd was a crew of men in tattered waders. One still clung to his fishing pole.

"Damn," Fisher said.

"You know them?" JD asked.

The man didn't reply, but the look on his face said that he did.

Woof rose.

"Fuck it. I ain't waiting around for the cops."

"What're you gonna do?" Fisher asked.

Woof trained the beam on the motorcycle JD had slammed his knee into.

"You're making a run for it?"

"I'm going for reinforcements."

JD was about to ask just what kind of reinforcements the man had in mind but the patch on Woof's vest spoke volumes. The Brothers of Boden were some real ass-kickin' motherfuckers. If Woof was rallying the troops, JD had a feeling they'd all be sporting leather.

"The Brothers...I mean, your friends," JD said. "Why not just call them?"

"Bastards aren't picking up."

"You're nuts," Fisher said, crawling to the hatch. He disappeared back down into the kitchen.

"What'd he say?" Woof asked, adjusting a squealing hearing aid.

"He said, 'Good Luck.'"

Back down in the bar, things had devolved into a series of shouting matches. Honey was busy laying into Chester for getting her roped into this mess, Doc was arguing with a couple of good old boys who were convinced it was all a prank, and Rowdy...Rowdy was chewing out the lot of them.

"Shut up, y'all!" JD's buddy hollered, the half-empty tequila bottle in his hand. "I can't hear myself drink."

The crowd shut up when they spotted Woof making his

way over to Doc. The bouncer whispered in Doc's ear, and Doc nodded solemnly.

"Would someone mind telling us what's going on? Is that so much to ask?" It was Chester. The guy was *really* starting to get on JD's nerves.

Doc held up a hand.

"Woof's going for help."

Murmured scoffs filled the room.

'If looks could kill' was a phrase JD had heard often enough but had never seen in action. The steely death gaze the bouncer gave the crowd ticked that box and then some.

"I need a distraction. Volunteers?"

JD could sense the collective reaction—mouths closed, eyes down.

The only one in the bar making any noise was Dubya. The dog thumped his tail joyfully, enjoying the piece of jerky Rowdy had stolen for him.

Woof took a deep breath.

"He'll do."

ELEVEN

"Bo, make them stop!"

Weena was practically in tears as JD and Woof strung the empty PBR cans to Dubya's collar.

"Doc wouldn't let 'em do it if he didn't think it would work," Bo said. "Would you, Doc?"

Doc was uncharacteristically silent.

Rowdy helped Fisher provide more empties—some of the beer going down the drain, some down Rowdy's gullet.

"That's ten cans," JD said as he leaned back to examine their handiwork. "Think that's enough?"

"It ain't gonna be your ass out there," Woof said. "I need him making as much noise as he can. Add a couple more."

By the time they finished, Dubya looked like a wedding getaway car. The final tally was twenty-four cans—a full case. The dog tried shaking his load loose. The resulting clatter would make for an effective distraction, JD had no doubt.

"You're gonna have to pry loose a few of those boards in back to let him out."

JD didn't relish the idea of exposing himself, even for the briefest of moments. But Woof wasn't directing his orders to anyone else—JD was his go-to guy.

"Can I have a moment with him?" Doc said.

Everyone looked uncomfortable as the old fellow knelt in front of his dog. He made a signal; Dubya sat. He held out his hand; Dubya shook.

"Be a good boy, okay?" Doc murmured, stroking the dog's head. "You run, you hear me? Run like the wind."

He nuzzled Dubya's muzzle, then glanced up at the onlookers. He wiped his nose and held out his hand to Woof.

The bouncer helped Doc to his feet.

"Let's do this."

Woof positioned himself at the front door with Bo on one side and Fisher on the other, both armed with screw guns. He gave a go signal, but before JD could lead Dubya to the back and into position, Honey surprised everyone.

"Got room on the back of that bike of yours?" she asked, stepping forward.

"Wait a minute. What do you think you're doing?" Chester complained. "Sorry, folks. Honey may be sweet, but sometimes—"

"Cut the bull, will you, Chester?"

"Excuse me?" Chester went red in the face.

"Oh, I'm sorry, is the gig still on? You think anyone in this shithole is interested in your shitty beer? Or has the gig been pretty much blown to hell? You want to fire me—fire me. But don't you dare order me around like you do her."

Honey pointed at Ruby, who suddenly found herself the unwanted center of attention.

"I paid for that costume," Chester sputtered.

"Unless you want me to strip in front of all these good folks, you're going to have to wait to get it back." She walked over to Woof and fixed her eyes on him. "Whaddya say, hoss?"

Woof simply nodded. He gave JD the 'go' signal.

Taking Dubya by the collar, JD walked the dog down the hallway to the back exit. Luis was waiting for him, hammer in hand, Doc having finally clued him in on the situation. The man was as nervous as a long-tail cat in a room full of rocking chairs.

"Tranquilo, Luis."

"Vete a la mierda, JD."

Dubya snarled at the door, causing both men to go silent. What if there was a sucker on the other side? What if there were more than one? Luis, JD decided, had every right to be nervous.

Bo appeared at the far end of the hall. He raised a finger, glancing back and forth between JD and the main bar section. JD understood. Woof would signal Bo; Bo would signal JD. He and Luis would open up a space small enough for the German Shepherd to crawl through, then Bo would give a final signal to Woof and Honey to start their run.

What could go wrong?

Bo gave the signal.

"Quita...esa...cosa," JD said, his Spanish failing him. He pointed at the bottom board covering the door.

Luis yanked a couple nails free and raised the board, creating a passthrough for Dubya. All JD had to do was reach through the planks, find the knob, open the door, and close it again as soon as the pooch made his exit.

Then, the dog whined.

JD looked down into Dubya's hazel eyes, and the plan crumbled like a stack of playing cards. The poor thing had no idea what it was in store for. How could he send it out there to possibly get torn to bits? There had to be another way.

Perhaps sensing his change of heart, Dubya planted a sloppy kiss on his cheek. No way was he sending the dog to its doom.

Luis threw up his hands in frustration.

And Bo mistook it as the signal.

"Go!" the young man shouted.

Shit. Shit, shit, shit!

"Wait!" JD cried, but as evidenced by the sound of the front door creaking open, he was too late.

Alarmed by the sudden chaos, Dubya bolted, running for the safety of his master. The plan was officially shot to hell.

He heard the front door slam shut followed by the whirr of screwdrivers. Woof and Honey were on their way, for better or worse.

Luis smacked JD in the head.

"¡Estúpido!"

"Yeah, that's me."

JD rose and dashed down the hall. He found Doc, his face buried in his dog's coat. The rest of the Saturday night crowd looked at JD in stunned disbelief. Apparently, Doc was the only one who was happy to see Dubya.

"You gotta be shittin' me," Fisher said, his mouth agape.

Everyone rushed to the windows, climbing over each other to peer through the crisscross of boards.

JD had no interest in looking. Whatever happened next was on him.

"They made it to the bike!" Bo cried.

A cheer rose from the crowd.

Somewhere beyond the walls of the bar, Honey screamed.

"Oh, fuck," someone moaned.

A distant squeal pierced the air. JD recognized it immediately.

Woof's damn hearing aids.

He joined the crowd and chanced a look through a slit in the boards. At first he couldn't see shit, then a flash of movement caught his eye.

It was Woof. The things had him, and they were dragging him off his motorcycle.

Through grease-stained glass, JD watched as the hulking fellow tried his best to fend off the suckers, which were increasing in number with every tick of the clock.

Honey watched as well, frozen on the back of the bouncer's bike. For the moment, the creatures were ignoring her, opting instead to go after the flailing tower of meat that was Woof.

But JD knew she didn't have long. As soon as the suckers had ripped the man's squealing ears from his head, they'd be on Honey like...well...like bears on honey.

A collective groan came from the bar as Woof toppled over, a majestic sequoia falling. As soon as the bouncer was down, it was feeding time at the Dockside parking lot. Suckers swarmed and blood sprayed.

The scream that rose from Woof's lips made JD turn away. What chance did any of them have if the toughest among them could be felled so easily?

Woof was toast, but Honey was still alive and kicking. Maybe there was still time to save the Huckleberry. JD looked over at Doc and Dubya. The dog was no longer an option—his master had already stripped him of the cans.

"Get ready to open that door," JD said. He strode over to Doc and retrieved the strung empties.

"Oh, no you don't," Rowdy protested.

JD gave him no heed. Instead, he shot Ruby a look.

"When they come for me, you get her inside."

Before she could answer, JD was already hightailing it down the hall. Luis met him at the back door.

"¿Dónde está el perro?"

"Yeah," JD said, motioning toward the door. "Open it."

TWELVE

By the time Luis ripped the last plank free, JD was having second thoughts.

This is crazy...

But there was no time to waste. Rowdy was already barreling down the hall, eager to put a stop to his mission.

"Speers, you nimrod! Get your sorry ass back here, pronto!"

"No can do, Kemosabe."

And with that, JD ducked through the hole Luis had provided.

The night air was still warm, and the scent of algae wafted his way from across the Mississippi to his left. It was the kind of night he loved, one you could get lost in as you wandered from tavern to pool hall to tavern, scoping out women and shooting the shit with friends you passed. June in Illinois was a blessing. That is, if you didn't have to try to lure a swarm of bloodsucking leech people your way.

He could see the creatures dogpiled atop Woof's body.

The feeding frenzy was in full swing. He could barely make out what the things were doing to the poor bouncer, the scene lit only by the glow of beer signs in the window, but that was probably for the best. From the sounds the swarming suckers were making, JD figured they had already dug deep into the man's entrails.

Honey was doing her best imitation of a statue, but he knew she was next on the menu.

JD swallowed, raised the string of cans up high, and shook them like shaking was going out of style.

"Woop! Woo-oop!" he cried.

The jangling cans made a powerful noise, and yet, when it came to catching the creatures' attention, their effect was zilch.

JD tried again.

"Come on, woop!"

Jangle-jangle.

"Woo-oop!"

Jangle-jangle.

"Let's go. Woo-oop!"

The look Honey threw him said it all. He was proving to be as ineffectual as a one-legged man in an ass-kicking contest.

JD ripped one of the empties free and threw it as hard as he could toward the swarm. Absent the heft of a filled can, the dead soldier landed far shy of its intended target.

He was stumped. Here he was, ripe for the picking, and the horde continued munching on the downed man. What did he have to do, send them an engraved invitation?

JD's phone went off in his pocket—an electronic version

of "Hollywood Nights" by one of his all-time favorites, Bob Seger & The Silver Bullet Band.

It was the ringtone he'd assigned to Kate's number.

"Not now!" he cried.

The woman's timing was nothing if not...

Hold on.

The warbling tune had gotten the suckers' attention. They raised their crimson-soaked faces from Woof's hollowed-out carcass. The Silver Bullet Band had succeeded where the PBR had not.

On they came, a collection of hikers, campers, trailer trash, and scouts, quivering strands of Woof's bloody intestines hanging from their mouths. There were even a few police officers in the mix, and JD realized that help wasn't on the way—it was already here. And it had a taste for human blood.

The first of the slavering things took a lurching step toward him—a postal carrier, from the look of her. She must have been bitten on the scalp because teeth sprouted from the top of her head like a tiara.

All right...bring it, you post office princess.

JD discarded the useless cans and dug his phone from his pocket. He raised it up, letting the music ring free, and a score of milky eyes followed. The monstrosities had all but abandoned Woof by now. JD and his portable tunes had their full attention.

"You got the keys?" he called out to Honey.

The woman on the bike wasn't taking any chances. She signaled JD with a single thumbs up.

The swarm moved as one, slowly at first, like the

cautious predators they were. But one by one, they separated from the growling crowd, as if they wanted to be the first to sink their legion of teeth into the fool holding aloft his outdated Samsung Galaxy.

JD held his ground—he had to time this just right. If the suckers were drawn by his phone, perhaps they'd follow it if he tossed it toward the brush. If not...

"I'll deal with that when I get there."

One...two...three...

His phone went silent.

His ex had hung up.

Thrown off by the sudden lack of ringtone, the mass of transmogrified people froze in place. Like sunflowers searching out the sun, they raised their heads, their hands, any body part now sporting a new mouth, and extended their teeth.

It was no trick of the light—their teeth were actually lengthening, in some cases past the point of any use for biting.

They're listening...

JD stood stock still. Honey sat, not making a move. Between them stood the crowd of drooling, twitching suckers, debating on their next move.

When Woof suddenly sat up, his entire chest cavity open and alive with teeth, Honey screamed her head off, sealing the deal. The creatures whirled on her, ready to strike.

It was split-second decision time. JD knew he usually came down on the wrong side of such choices, like when his buddy Ken had offered him a free ticket to see the Zac Brown Band the same night as his anniversary. The ticket was going, going, gone, and choosing badly had marked the beginning of his and Kate's slow slide into marital disharmony.

The way to the back of the bar was clear. He could haul ass and be safely back inside lickety-split, no harm, no foul. Who could blame him?

Me, that's who.

"Thanks for nothing!" Honey yelled, doing her best to extract herself from the bike.

"Stay put!" JD called back.

His feet flew into action before his brain did. He cut a wide arc around the snarling multitude, betting on his ability to outrun the suckers. A large number had been perambulatorily impaired, leg bones bent and jutting, the result no doubt of the attack on their person.

Person. What a strange word, he thought. Because none of the wretches here in the parking lot were people, save for Honey and him. The rest were shambling meat husks, hosts for whatever nastiness had taking a liking for the human form and crawled on inside.

JD leaped over a log, which he suddenly realized was not a log at all—it was poor ol' Larry's left half. It wriggled across the grass in a horrible imitation of an inchworm. JD made it a point not to look back.

Woof rode an old, restored Harley—at least he had before he was eaten alive. It was plastered with faded stickers and sported twin saddle bags. It was truly a work of art, but all JD cared about was whether or not he could get it running.

The last time he'd been on a bike was with his dad. The man, as usual, was liquored up when he tried to teach his ten-year-old how to ride. With his father squashed up behind him, his hot beer breath on his son's neck, JD had done his best to keep the Kawasaki "Widowmaker" on the road. He'd failed, the Speers boys had ended up in a ditch, and he couldn't sit down for a week from the whipping the old man had given him.

Honey urged him on.

JD hopped aboard the Harley. The woman was right—Woof had gotten so far as to insert his key into the ignition. A rabbit's foot hung from the keychain.

Good. We're gonna need all the luck we can get.

"Hang on."

Honey threw her arms around him and pressed in tight.

JD turned the ignition. The bike gave a roar before settling into a steady *chop-chop-chop*. He gripped the throttle and urged the hog forward with his feet.

They were on the move.

Unfortunately, so were the suckers.

Some of the creatures were quite nimble. JD even caught sight of one that was nothing but a torso and arms chasing after them like some kind of nightmarish chicken.

A trio of scouts ambushed them not ten yards from the bar. The mutated kiddies pounced, one grabbing for Honey, another leaping into the path of the oncoming bike.

JD hit the gas. The scout in the headlight, festooned with merit badges and teeth, didn't even try to get out of the way. JD didn't so much as blink as he ran him over. The thing reaching for Honey met its end beneath the bike's rear wheel.

Two down, one to go. But where the hell was the last boy scout?

He threw a look back and got his answer. The young'un

was latched onto one of the saddlebags, teeth chewing away at the leather.

The Dockside was coming up fast. There was no time to try to shake the kid loose.

"This is gonna suck," he said, warning Honey of his intentions.

"Fuck me," Honey moaned.

JD laid on the horn. If anyone was standing on the other side of the door, they'd better move, and fast.

The bike hit the single cement step leading to the door, and for a moment the motorcycle was airborne.

If only the old man could see me now...

The thrill was short lived.

They hit the door with a vengeance—it swung open and off its hinges.

The folks inside the bar scattered. The only person close enough to be in any real danger was Chester, and it registered with JD that taking him out would be no great loss.

He hit the brakes and the bike skidded sideways across the floor, rubber squealing against linoleum. The jukebox was coming up fast, but there was no stopping the Harley's forward momentum.

Time to jump.

With Honey still wrapped about him like a sweet potato vine, JD leaned far to the left, giving up his hold on the hog. The two of them tumbled headlong into a four-top, while the bike, scout in tow, took out Ruby's cutout and the beer trough before slamming into the Wurlitzer.

JD rammed the table's edge with his forehead, splitting skin and probably costing him none too few brain cells. Honey was luckier—she slid under the table entirely, taking out chairs like bowling pins, before coming to a stop at Rowdy's feet.

The last thing JD heard before he clocked out was Woof's Harley hitting home, colliding with the jukebox and setting Tennessee Ernie Ford a'croonin'.

THIRTEEN

JD drifted in a fog. He saw Kate, his ex, swimming naked in a pool filled with koi, giant kittens watching from the water's edge, poised to swipe at the flickering fish. Kate caught him staring and shook her head.

"Wake up, Speers."

JD opened his eyes. Rowdy loomed over him.

"Here, drink this."

His friend fed him a shot. JD coughed and spat out the tequila, pushing Rowdy away.

"You trying to kill me?" JD sputtered.

"Well, *that's* a waste of some good Reposado, right there."

JD sat up. He could sense time had fast forwarded while he was out, but he couldn't tell how much—his internal clock was on the fritz. He was coming back around, but not as quick as he would like.

"How's Honey?"

"She's fine," Rowdy assured him. "A little banged up, but no worse for the wear. That's one tough gal."

"Weena!" Doc called. "Crank the smoke eater. It smells like the devil's armpit in here."

Weena flipped a switch, and an ancient air purification system kicked in with a cough.

Rowdy nodded toward the motorcycle. "You took out a dozen cases of that Huckleberry swill when you hit. That stuff stinks to high heaven."

"Help me up, would you?"

Rowdy obliged, hoisting JD to his feet. The room played Tilt-a-Whirl. But as soon he regained his equilibrium, he could see the scene more clearly.

His eyes first lit on the front entrance, fearful as he was of the gaping hole he'd left when he Evel Knieveled his way into the bar. But no, the door was back in place, held firm by a patchwork of planks.

"Any get inside?"

"Just the one you rode in with. And things have gone quiet outside. Those critters have either moved on or they're bidin' their time. I for one ain't gonna risk stickin' my neck out to see."

JD glanced about the room. Ruby's mangled cutout lay on the floor amidst a wash of ice and broken beer bottles. The Harley was toast, its twisted frame enmeshed with the inner workings of the jukebox. The Wurlitzer had spun its last tune.

Across the room, Doc and some others busied themselves over something atop the bar. With their backs to him, blocking his view, he couldn't make out what had them so preoccupied. Dubya sat at Doc's feet, looking up at the goings-on with rapt attention.

"Think you used up a few of your nine lives, my friend."

JD cracked his neck. Pain as sharp as an icepick speared his head. His buddy steadied him.

"Take it slow. Why don't you stay down a spell longer?"

JD obeyed.

"Once you get your bearings, you gotta go see what Doc's up to."

"Can't you just tell me?"

"It's better if you see it."

"Come on, Rowdy."

The man stroked his beard. "What do you remember about your big entrance?"

"Stop doing that!"

"Doing what?"

"Drawing things out for effect. Just fucking tell me already."

"Fine!" Rowdy huffed. "That kid what latched onto the bike? Dead as a doornail. Doc and them's got him trussed up on the bar. Doc's fixin' to do some sorta autopsy on him. See what makes 'em tick."

"Jesus."

Rowdy clapped his friend on the back. "That was a brave thing you done. Stupid as hell, but brave."

"Didn't really have a choice."

"Yeah, you did. I saw what you done." Rowdy wiggled his eyebrows. "So did she."

JD wrinkled his brow. "She who?"

"Mind if I have a minute?"

JD turned to find Ruby standing before him, a bottle of water in her hand.

"I thought you could use something a little less potent," she said, eyeing the empty shot glass in Rowdy's hand.

"I'll leave you to it." And with that, his friend was off to join the folks crowded around the bar.

"Thanks for saving Hailey."

JD quirked his head. Had he heard correctly? "Hailey?"

"Sorry. Honey."

"Honey?" JD's mind was swimming. Was he about to start seeing giant kittens again too?

"Honey is just a name on a costume."

JD looked down at the embroidered *R-U-B-Y* on her chest.

"You really don't remember me, do you?" Ruby shook her head. "I thought you were playing, but..." She smiled, but there was a hint of hurt in it. "Guess I didn't make a very big impression."

Not Ruby. *Not* Ruby. His brain processed the information, but still he was no closer to the answer than...

"Tru?"

The name popped out of his mouth unbidden. Ruby—no, *not* Ruby, Tru—chuckled.

"So, you *do* remember."

Trudy Worth. Jesus Christ, it was Trudy Worth.

"Holy..." It was all JD got out before Chester interrupted them.

"You two look pretty chummy."

Chummy. The guy was the worst.

"Just thanking our hero," Ruby...no, Trudy said.

Chester grinned. "Hero? I guess that's one word for it. Not sure the bouncer would agree."

"Chester—"

"Oh, calm down, Ruby." The man's tone was so patronizing that he might as well run for Congress.

"You mean Trudy, don't you?" JD stood.

The grin faded from Chester's face, revealing the stone-faced asshole he really was.

"I thought we were clear about keeping a certain distance from the clientele." He was speaking to Trudy but his eyes were trained on JD. And there was that pissy tone again.

"That's what you're worried about, Chester? This place is surrounded by things that want to rip us apart, and *that's* what you're worried about?"

"Easy, Ruby—"

"Fuck you."

Chester pulled back, one hand upraised. Whether or not the douche would have actually followed through was anybody's guess, but JD made sure he never got the chance. He grabbed the man by the wrist and stepped in close.

"I know guys like you." JD mimicked Chester's punchable grin. "Heck, I've *been* guys like you."

"Not sure I catch your meaning, friend." Chester's calm words and demeanor belied the temper bubbling to the surface. The man certainly had a short fuse.

"We're both pieces of shit," JD told the man. "Thing is, I own it. You? You're goddamn clueless."

"Come on, Chester, let's—"

Chester didn't let her finish. He held up his left hand—a silver band inset with a large jewel glittered in the light.

"See this?" Gone was any sign of the slick salesman. The *real* Chester was in the house. "This ring of mine is worth more than your entire miserable life."

"Good for you, Liberace. Did you get a matching one for your cock?"

JD always knew when he had pushed another man too far. It was one of his very limited special skills. There was a certain weight to the final words before fists flew. And the zinger he'd just dropped had some heft.

Chester's attack was as unconventional as his necktie—an oversized bolo with a little beer bottle at the center. Instead of throwing a punch, the man reached out and grabbed him by the ear—the ear with the bits of buckshot still embedded within the flesh—and squeezed.

Fireworks exploded in JD's lobe.

JD screamed.

Chester obviously wasn't satisfied with his first effort. He squeezed again, harder this time, and JD felt something pop. A couple pellets of buckshot hit the floor, along with a splat of his blood.

JD stumbled backward, and as he did so, the bastard finally released his grip, a broad, satisfied smile on his lips. JD reached for his ear—the lobe was torn clean in two. It felt like hot deli meat. An image of Larry splitting in half leaped into his mind.

JD tried to curse, but only managed, "Ear! You!"

"That's enough!"

Doc stepped away from the bar, his hands stained with the scout's blood. The room fell silent.

"Speers! My office. Now!"

Doc sat JD down in the desk chair and closed the office door. A giant mounted walleye stared down at them, ready for the fun to commence. The place was littered with papers: bills, flyers, you name it—some stacked in piles on the desk, others tacked to the wall. Whatever semblance of order Doc kept in the bar proper, he abandoned here in his office.

"Just can't keep your nose clean, can you?" Doc rummaged around in a metal cabinet covered in magnets advertising medicines for pets, remnants of his veterinarian days.

"My nose ain't the issue, Doc."

Doc extracted a mason jar filled with pickled eggs. "Want one?"

The eggs looked like they'd been pickled sometime in the last century. It was a hard pass for JD.

"No thanks."

"Suit yourself." Doc popped the top, and gas escaped, perfuming the room with Eau de Fart. He extracted a gray egg and swallowed it down.

Doc pulled out a bottle of iodine and doused JD's ear before he knew what was happening. The move so shocked JD that he forgot to scream. It was like the man had just dipped his earlobe into boiling cooking oil.

"Sit still." Doc set aside the bottle and quickly threaded a surgical needle. To say JD felt woozy would be to do a disservice to the word. "Concentrate on something else."

JD placed his attention on the calendar hanging on the wall across the room. February 1999—an oldie but a goodie. The fourteenth was circled in red, the name Wilhelmina scrawled within its box. Doc was single, as far as JD knew, so the old fellow's Valentine's date must have been a bust.

The needle pierced skin, JD shrieked. By the time Doc was done stitching, JD was well and truly hoarse.

"Not my best work, but it'll do. I've seen cats who hold still better than you."

JD was at a loss for words. His earlobe was a raging ball of fire.

Doc opened the mini-fridge next to his desk, rooted around, and came up with a jar filled with muddy water. Lazing about in the water were little wormy creatures.

"Gonna have to get the blood flowing or that lobe of yours is gonna turn black and fall off."

"What are those?" JD asked, peering cautiously at the jar.

"What do they look like?" Doc replied, fishing out a few leeches.

JD scooted back in his chair. "I don't think so."

"Tough shit," Doc said. He selected the liveliest of the batch and held it to JD's ear. "Doctor's orders."

There was no pain as the thing latched on, only an uncomfortable tug. JD reached up to touch it, and Doc swatted his hand away.

"Leave it."

Great, just great. He'd managed to avoid the suckers outside only to become intimately acquainted with them here in Doc's office.

"For how long?" JD asked.

Doc didn't reply. He was staring at the remaining leeches in his palm.

"Well, I'll be..."

He tipped his hand, and the leeches dropped back into the jar.

"It wasn't my fault, Doc."

"That's interesting..."

"That man out there is a psychopath—"

Doc shushed him.

"You okay, Doc?"

The man just grinned and shook the jar like some sort of grim snow globe.

"I think this old boy just figured something out."

FOURTEEN

Weena buried her face in Bo's chest as Doc Moser attacked the scout's mouth with a scalpel.

"I can't watch!"

Rowdy was hogging the view. JD wriggled past him to get a better look.

"New earring?" Rowdy asked, eyeing the leech hanging from JD's ear.

"Fuck you."

Doc had a captive audience. Everyone—save for Chester, who brooded alone in a corner—had gathered around him, eager to see what the man had in store. Doc had left the office in a rush, some brilliant notion abuzz in his noggin, and gone straight for the dead scout. His excitement was palpable.

The old vet sawed away at the corpse lying on the bar. The kid was dressed in the same scouting outfit as the rest of the swarm that had attacked them back on County 3 after they'd run the Huckleberries off the road.

Upon closer inspection, the badges on the boy's chest

didn't resemble any JD had ever seen. The majority were crucifix-themed. One appeared to show Jesus playing...volleyball?

As he stared, the boy belched. Everyone took a step back.

"Easy, everyone. Just a bit of gas."

Doc pressed the corpse's stomach to make his point. The dead sucker burped again, this time releasing a spew of brown liquid.

"Aw, God!" Rowdy said. "Is that blood?"

Doc sniffed its open mouth, then made a quick search of the dead boy's pockets. He pulled out an orange wrapper.

"Peanut butter cups."

This was too much for Weena. She bolted for the restroom. Bo looked like he wanted to stay and watch the dissection, yet he followed her to the back.

"A little fast for decomposition, wouldn't you say, Doc?" Fisher asked.

"Not necessarily," Doc explained, prying open the sucker's jaws with a medical instrument that looked to JD like run-of-the-mill pliers. "Something's breaking the body down from within. Enzymes and such. I'm guessing the last time this boy drew breath was hours ago. See his pallor? Blue as all get out. But that's not what's got me interested..."

Doc latched onto one of the teeth sprouting from the angry mouth and yanked it free. A collective sphincter clench rippled through the crowd. He held the tooth up to the light.

"Let's see if I'm right..."

Bo found Weena sobbing in one of the stalls of the women's restroom. She was inconsolable.

"Hey, Hon. Everything's gonna be okay."

Weena looked up at him, her running mascara making her look like she had two black eyes. Bo wiped away the smudges.

"It's just..." she hiccupped, "you know, ever since Sammy..."

Sammy was Weena's little brother—the kid had an devastating accident on a camping trip about a decade earlier. Their father had been chopping firewood when the hatchet he was using slipped out of his hands. Sometimes, in the middle of the night, Weena could still see him, a hot dog in his hand, the hatchet blade in his forehead.

Bo stepped into the stall with her and wrapped his arms around her.

"I know, I know."

Bo kissed away her tears. She slowly put her arms around his neck.

The next thing they knew, they were necking.

The parking lot was oddly empty of suckers, or so it seemed. The Airstream sat at an angle, still hooked to Rowdy's pickup which remained burrowed into the back of Chester's Ram. The horde was nowhere to be seen at present. Whether they were lying low or had moved on to find easier pickings was anybody's guess.

The crickets sure as hell didn't know—they sang on as if

this were any old Saturday evening at the Dockside, which for them, it was.

All was still in the parking lot.

Except for a lone figure rolling through the grass, slowly making its way toward the tavern.

If Doc's had security cameras, someone might have spotted the intruder, but Doc put a high price on freedom— his own and that of his customers.

So, when Larry's left half rolled up to the bar and burrowed through its rotting foundation, there was no one to warn the crew inside.

Half-Larry had abandoned his right side. It lay at the bottom of a ditch, unable to extract itself. But his left was on the move, crawling along on toothy tendrils, digging into the cool earth to propel itself forward...forward.

At last the halved corpse found what it was looking for: the jury-rigged collection of pipes that served as the Dockside's plumbing. Its lone eye surveyed the crisscross of conduits and found one to its liking. An awkward one-handed pushup later, the sucker was face-to-face with a wide, corroded sewer pipe. Stretching upward as far as it could, tendons snapping with the effort, it bit down on the metal and began to chew.

One tooth broke through, then another. The sensitive nerves within its fangs could sense the sewage within. The perfect entry point.

Half-Larry flexed and released, flexed and released, with all the fervor of a frog leg being electrified by a high school biology student. Injecting its essence into the pipe.

The partial corpse collapsed. Spent. And crumpled into nothing but a husk.

But its task was complete.

"See, I got a theory," Doc began. "If these things are anything like leeches—"

Before he could continue, Chester rose from his chair.

"Listen, I don't know about y'all, but it sounds pretty quiet out there to me." Folks shushed him, but he continued. "As much as I'd like to hang around and watch you play *Operation*, I'm ready to cut my losses and go."

"Go, then," Trudy said.

JD smiled.

"Don't think I won't," Chester warned.

"Would you *please* be quiet," Doc snapped. "I think I figured something out, but I need to test it. So, shut... your...trap!"

Weena broke away from Bo, twisting sideways to extract herself from the bathroom stall.

"What's wrong?" Bo asked. Making out with Weena was exactly the sort of distraction he could use right now.

"I can't get that boy out of my head. What Doc's doing to him is—"

"He's dead, Weena." Bo hadn't meant to put it so bluntly.

The effect of his words was instantaneous.

"That doesn't mean they get to cut him up!"

"C'mon," Bo said, trying to salvage the situation. "That's not Sammy out there."

Weena face tightened and she stabbed Bo in the chest with her finger. "It might as well be! Sammy was a sco-out!" She howled the last bit, ragged breaths shaking her small frame.

There was no going back. Not right now. Damn.

"Why don't you go get yourself a pop, huh, Hon? Might make you feel better."

Weena jabbed him with her finger once more for good measure and stalked out of the room, letting the door slam on her way out.

Ah, well. Perhaps trying to get it on with Weena under these circumstances wasn't one of his best ideas. When they got out of here, he'd take her on a proper date, flowers and all. He thought he remembered her saying that she loved lilies. He could pick some up at Flowers by Frank and then take her across the river to the Big Muddy. They made a good steak, as he recalled.

But first, he had to take a leak.

He should probably hold it until he swapped bathrooms, but when you gotta go, you gotta go.

He quickly unzipped and soon had a steady stream going. That was the thing about beer—you didn't buy it, you rented it.

Bo glanced over at the graffitied wall, curious how it stacked up to the filth scrawled in the men's room. A little poem caught his eye.

> Here I sit, at a loss,
> Trying to shit out taco sauce.

It wasn't Shakespeare, but then again, Bo didn't know any Shakespeare, and the rhyme made him laugh.

Had he looked down instead of rereading the little poem, he might have noticed that his stream of urine had gone dark brown. Not starting at its source, but coming up from the bowl. Something was making its way upward through his urine, like salmon swimming upstream to spawn.

When the darkness reached its highest point, the stream suddenly stopped. Bo felt a bite where no man would ever hope to feel one.

Then, everything went red.

Chester headed for the front entrance. He grabbed a cordless drill off a stool and gave the trigger a squeeze.

Rowdy took to the floor.

"You remove one of them boards, and you can bet your granny's ass I'll beat you over the head with it."

"Good one, Rowdy," JD said.

"Thanks."

Chester aimed the drill at Rowdy. "I'd like to see you try." He gave it another squeeze for good measure.

Trudy stomped her foot. "Give it a break, Chester!"

"Yeah," Hailey echoed, "Stop acting like a child!"

Chester fumed. "You ungrateful...you'll never work in the beer business again, either of you!"

"Fine with me!" Hailey shouted. "I was sick of shilling for your sour ass beer anyway."

This seemed to piss Chester off more than anything so far. "Don't you disparage my beer!"

Weena slipped back into the room. She looked about, sensing the change in the weather. "What's going on?"

Rowdy upped the ante by unsheathing his knife. "This fellow's fixin' to sing soprano."

Doc waved his arms. He'd lost all control over the situation.

"Be quiet!" he cried. "I think I figured out how to beat these bastards at their own game, so will you all just—"

Doc stopped mid-sentence. His mouth twitched.

JD turned. *Is the old guy having a stroke.*

That was when he noticed Bo was back. Maybe it was the boy's weekend warrior skills, but he'd done a fine job of sneaking up behind Doc unseen.

But now JD noticed—oh, shit, did he notice.

"Just...just...just..." Doc stammered.

Bo had turned.

And he had his teeth buried deep in the back of Doc's head.

"Doc?" JD whispered.

Bo sucked mightily. Doc's face went white, his cheeks sinking into hollows, his eyes disappearing into his skull.

"Doc?"

Bo reversed the flow. Doc's face swelled like a red balloon.

Jesus Christ, he's gonna blow...

And just like that, Doc's head exploded in a shower of blood and bone and gore.

FIFTEEN

The leech dangling from JD's ear, having drunk its fill, detached and fell to the floor with an unceremonious plop.

So did Doc. Minus his head.

Dubya howled, and Chester screamed.

Whatever big idea Doc had about stopping the suckers in their tracks was gone with the wind.

Bo stood in the center of the room, a snarling, snapping thing of pure hunger. JD watched as the last of the color drained from the young guy's eyes. Strips of Doc's scalp hung from Bo's teeth. His hands twitched and snapped, bones shifting within, distorting them into talons. JD couldn't help but stare. A real-life late night creature feature was playing out in front of his eyes.

"Bo!"

Standing behind the boy as she was, Weena hadn't gotten a good look at the beast Bo had turned into. But when the sucker whirled on her, she got a *damn* good look. Bo bit down on her face, creating a ghoulish imitation of their regular Saturday night necking sessions. Weena's eyes went white as Bo drank. The resultant slurping sounds made JD gag.

"Watch it, Speers!" Rowdy was pointing frantically. JD followed his gaze.

Doc's headless body was moving. The blood spurting from the top of his neck went frothy, then sputtered like an aerosol can losing its steam. The first tooth emerged, followed by hundreds more—a crimson mouth blossoming where the old vet's noggin used to be.

JD stepped back as Doc's legs drummed the floor like he'd taken up Irish step dancing in death. One swift swipe of his left foot, and JD discovered he hadn't stepped back far enough. Doc's foot connected, and JD went sprawling.

Dang it!

Doc's body sat up the same moment JD did. It was going to be a race to see which one of them could get verticle first. JD scrambled valiantly, his shoes slipping in the pool of blood on the floor. Doc's body simply hopped up, going from sitting to standing in a single move that would have impressed even the most cynical of Olympic judges. JD gave the sucker a twelve out of ten.

"Don't do it," JD said, eyeing up the headless corpse. It responded with a gurgle from deep in its chest that exited its new mouth with a noxious spray, like bloody breath escaping a harpooned whale's blowhole.

Then, the sucker rushed him.

There was a reason JD never played football in high school. He'd tried out because his father had insisted upon it, but during his first practice, JD cracked three ribs and dislocated his thumb. He simply froze up when the linebackers charged.

It was déjà vu all over again.

The creature that had stolen Doc's body moved faster than it should have been able to—pushing its new legs to the limit. The thing plowed into JD, bowling him over, reacquainting him with the gore-stained floor.

JD squeezed his eyes shut, certain that after his tumble came the teeth. But when he looked up, he saw that Doc's body had no interest in him.

It was barreling toward the front door.

Oh, shit.

"Sonofabitch..." Rowdy said.

Doc's body hit the door with tremendous force, the sound of breaking bones and wood intermingling. And he was gone, out the door and into the night.

Dubya gave one last bark and chased after his dead master.

"Get back here!" JD cried, but the dog had made its mind up. Hasta la vista, Dubya.

There was a fleeting moment when JD thought perhaps the worst was over. But then a swarm of suckers appeared in the open doorway, taking JD's hopes, dashing them to the ground, and mashing them underfoot.

In the split second before JD threw himself over the bar, he took a mental snapshot of the horde. Pale and bloated, the suckers crowded the doorway as if someone had just announced last call. Overstretched lips made way for jutting teeth. And the sound they made was equal parts human and nonhuman—halfway between cries of agony and famished growls.

The logjam broke, the suckers toppled into the tavern, and JD scrambled up and over the bar. He landed on something soft.

"Jesus!"

JD lifted himself up and came face-to-face with an embroidered breast. *H-O-N-E-Y,* the breast read.

"If you're done reading my tit, get off," Hailey said.

"Sorry."

Trudy was the next to tumble over the bar. She missed JD and landed squarely on Hailey, knocking the wind out of her for a second time.

"This just ain't my day," Hailey croaked.

"Watch yourselves back there!" Rowdy cried. "Incoming!"

JD braced for impact as Rowdy, his arm around Fisher's waist, rolled over the bar top and dropped. Luckily, neither one of the men landed on those already in hiding. Rowdy bounced when he hit; Fisher fell like a rock.

"How is it out there?" JD asked.

"Like coupon day at the Sizzler," Rowdy said. "If you ain't on this side of the bar, you're dead meat."

Chester screamed again.

"Guess the man's calling you a liar," JD said.

Trudy crawled over to JD, careful to keep her head down. "Chester's still out there."

"So I gather."

"We've got to help him out!"

JD laughed. "Risk my neck for that asshole? Not likely."

"Yeah, he's an asshole. But he doesn't deserve to die."

"You sure about that?"

Trudy grabbed him by the collar and pulled out the big

guns. "Prom 2011. You left me on the dancefloor in the middle of "Honky Tonk Stomp" and never came back. Remember that? I cried for weeks, I was so embarrassed."

Shame flooded over JD, coloring his cheeks red. No wonder he'd had such a hard time placing her. On the day of the prom, he'd been three sheets to the wind by four-thirty. Phil Peppers, Big Tim, and he had busted into Phil's father's liquor cabinet. The man had a taste for drinks involving cream liqueurs, and the pre-game cookies JD tossed were as sweet as cupcakes. By the time he finally got around to picking up Trudy in his old Dodge, he was barely aware of his own name.

Had he really left this beautiful woman alone on the dancefloor? What a jackass.

"You owe me."

JD sighed. The road was forking once more. Turn left, stay safe, maybe make it out of this night alive; turn right...

He spied an old baseball bat shoved to the back of a shelf filled with highball glasses. He'd only seen Doc wield it once when some real skid marks from Sheboygan had tried to rob the place. The guys had been high on whatever they got high on up in Wisconsin, and one look at Doc waving the bat and screaming like a deranged Babe Ruth sent them running.

JD grabbed the bat. Burned into the wood were the words *Shock and Awe.*

Rowdy looked stunned. "You ain't actually going out there?"

"I say we beat 'em back long enough to give ol' Chester a chance, then we get the hell outta here."

"Yeah?" Rowdy groaned. "And go where?"

"I haven't got that part quite figured out yet."

"Doc's got a boat," Fisher said.

"Haven't got it figured out yet? That's a pretty fuckin' big piece of the puzzle, don't you think?"

"I'm working on it, I'm working on it!"

"It's just a little jon boat, but he keeps it docked out back," Fisher said.

"Well, I for one ain't riskin' my hide on your half-baked plan!"

"Boys!" Hailey scream-whispered. She pointed her thumb at Fisher. "Are you hearing this?"

"What?" JD asked.

"Doc's got a boat docked out back," Fisher said.

Once the info finally sank in, JD leaned over and kissed Fisher on the forehead. "My man!"

"That's a long fuckin' run to the dock," Rowdy said. "We gotta get down the hall, through the door, down the ramp—"

"You'd rather stay here?"

"No, JD, I would not. I'm just sayin'—"

JD held up a finger. "We're going."

"Man," Rowdy moaned. He reached for a couple bottles of house liquor, tossed them aside upon finding them to be plastic, and chose instead a bottle of Jack Daniels and bottle of Jim Beam. He held them at the neck, brandishing them like clubs. "If I'm clockin' out, I'm gonna have my buddies Jack and Jim with me."

"You ready?" JD asked.

"Not in the slightest."

"Alright." JD tightened his grip. "Batter up."

Hurling himself over the bar was a lot easier than climbing atop it. In the first instance, he'd had momentum and adrenaline on his side; this time, gravity and reluctance weighed him down. JD rose, planted his right foot on top of the ice trough, and pushed himself up with his left. The metal trough shifted under his weight, and one of its legs bent under the pressure. Ice spilled down on Fisher's head.

JD caught his balance. He raised the bat, ready to do battle.

Where the hell is Chester?

The man was nowhere to be seen. Just a sea of swaying suckers, their eyes—and mouths—focused on him. JD suddenly felt like the lone stripper at a bachelor party.

He wasn't alone for long. With much heaving and cursing, Rowdy joined him on top of the bar. When Rowdy stood, he was as shocked as his friend.

"Where is the douchebag?"

"Fuck if I know," JD replied. He swung the bat golf club-style, cracking a pizza delivery man's skull.

"I'd give my left nut for a Colt 45 right about now, and I ain't talkin' malt beverage," Rowdy said as he brought the Jack down on a barfly's head. "Where the hell's all the guns?"

JD nodded at the drooling crowd. "They got 'em."

Rowdy quickly assessed the throng. To a man, everybody packing heat had been suckerfied.

"Shit."

A pair of smoldering creatures reached for Rowdy's boot. The two appeared to have been police officers in their previous life. By the look of the third-degree burns covering their bodies, it was apparent their prowler had gone up in flames. The heat from the fire must have fused them together, melting fat intermingling. Now they moved as one.

A joke his father used to tell popped into his head.

"What's worse than a cop in your rearview mirror?"

"What, Daddy?"

"Two cops!"

It wasn't much of a joke, but then again, Roger Speers wasn't much of a father.

"You gotta be kiddin' me!" Rowdy shouted.

JD smacked away another sucker before spotting the source of Rowdy's wrath.

Chester was hoofing it down the hall toward the kitchen. Luis stood in the doorway, frantically waving the man in.

"Looks like the joke's on us," Rowdy snarled.

JD sighed.

Ain't it always?

SIXTEEN

"Look alive, Speers!" Rowdy shouted. His buddy walloped Bo with the Jim Beam, sending teeth scattering. "Sorry, Bo!"

"We gotta get to the kitchen," JD said.

"What happened to the boat?"

"We're going, we're going. Just gonna get there in stages, that's all."

"Why?"

JD nodded toward the hallway. Even at this distance, it was clear to see that suckers were pounding and chewing their way through the back door. The rear exit was a no-go.

"Shit," Rowdy moaned.

"No worries. We get to the kitchen, duck out the window, and *boom*—we're off to the races."

JD caught sight of an arm crawling through the front door—mouth in the middle of its hand. It bit, dragged, bit, dragged. The sight of it was enough to drive a man insane.

"That kitchen even have a window?" Rowdy asked.

JD didn't have a clue. "Sure it does."

He swung again, knocking back a miserable creature with mouths where her ears should have been. His follow-through caught the oldest living landline this side of the Mississippi and sent it flying toward Rowdy's head.

"Watch it, Sammy Sosa!"

JD addressed the folks hiding behind the bar. "We're going to make a run for the kitchen."

"Why not make a run for the back door?" Fisher asked.

"Because I say so, that's why." JD didn't mention that any attempt at the door would lead to certain death. Best to keep the ball rolling.

"You sure about this?" Trudy looked up at him warily.

"One hundred percent." JD turned to Rowdy. "Toss me your lighter."

"I gave up smokin' last year, you know that."

"Yeah? Well, why's your truck always smell like Camels? Toss it over!"

Rowdy stuck the bottle of Jack under his arm, freeing up his hand to fish around in his pocket. He came up with his Zippo and flipped it to JD.

"Now, douse this bar with booze."

"Jesus, you're gonna get us killed!"

JD spotted Weena. Once timid in demeanor, this new, twisted version of the young woman was anything but—round mouth open to its fullest, gullet flexing, teeth bared and eager to chomp down. JD delivered a swift kick to her forehead, and she tumbled back into the swarming crowd.

"Do it!"

"Alright!"

Rowdy unscrewed the caps on both bottles and poured out the booze. Soon, the bar top was awash in whiskey.

"Ready?" JD asked, flicking open the lighter and igniting the flame.

"Not in the fucking slightest."

JD called back to Trudy. "When I say go, go!"

He threw up a prayer to heaven, hoping to God that God would hear it, and dropped the blazing lighter.

The Zippo landed dead center in the pooling liquor. And with a hiss, it went out.

"What the...?"

"Well, *that* was a big ol' bust," Rowdy said.

"I don't understand," JD stammered, snatching up the lighter and shaking it. "It works in the movies."

"This ain't the movies, kid."

A raft of growling Grim Reapers ready to slurp up human blood? Sure looked like the movies to him. But Rowdy was right—it was time for a new plan.

JD pocketed the Zippo and assessed the situation. It was a clear shot from behind the bar to the hallway leading to the kitchen—if only he could get the suckers to move in the opposite direction. If only...

His eyes lit upon an object hanging on the far wall. What had been meant as a gag gift from Fisher had become a permanent fixture of the Dockside. He only hoped the batteries weren't dead.

"Rowdy!" JD shouted. "Aim for Billy!"

"Wha?"

JD pointed frantically. "Billy!"

Rowdy looked in the direction his friend was pointing. JD wasn't sure the man had picked up what he was laying down, but when Rowdy wound up for the pitch, Jim Beam bottle at the ready, he knew he had.

Rowdy let the bottle fly.

It hit the framed Big Mouth Billy Bass hard. The rubber fish lurched to life, a tiny speaker squeaking out the words to, "Take Me To The River." The novelty fish's mouth moved, and its tail flapped. A bargain at forty bucks.

The reaction was everything JD had hoped for and then some. A room full of heads snapped toward the singing fish on the wall. And then, the horde rushed it, climbing over each other to try to get the first taste of the flapping thing. They snapped at each other like starving dogs, and the best part about it was they instantly had *zero* interest in the two fools standing on the bar.

"Go, go, go!" JD cried.

Trudy gave her fellow Huckleberry a shove, and Hailey in turn shoved Fisher. The three double-timed it as they scrambled from behind the safety of the bar and made a dash for the kitchen.

"That means you too," JD said to Rowdy.

"You don't have to tell me twice."

The two men dashed down the bar top toward the hallway, knocking over drinks and upending bowls of nuts. The edge was fast approaching—JD didn't slow a bit. He made the leap, holding the bat out before him like a lightsaber.

Damn, I bet I look cool.

The feeling was short-lived. He came down hard on his heel and felt his ankle buckle. Pain shot up his calf, stopping him in his tracks.

He'd forgotten Rowdy was on his heels.

The big man plowed into him, having bellyflopped off the bar in his eagerness to escape the horde. JD heard his ankle *pop*.

The two tumbled end over end into the hall, bouncing off walls, knocking framed photos to the floor with an earsplitting crash.

Judging by the gurgling howl that rose from the swarm, the two men were instantly more interesting than a rubber bass. JD and Rowdy were back on the menu.

Rowdy was the first to his feet—for a big guy, the sonofabitch could move. He did have moonshiner blood in him, after all.

Rowdy was down the hall and to the kitchen door before JD was even to his feet.

"C'mon!" Rowdy urged him on.

JD hobbled as fast as he could toward his friend's outstretched hand. He could feel the creatures stumbling after him, but he had no interest in looking back. The skin on the back of his neck prickled, anticipating the bite that would take him out.

He reached out with the bat, and Rowdy took it, pulling him in, the two of them tumbling through the kitchen door.

Luis slammed the door shut behind them and slid the latch in place. A second later, a set of teeth plunged through the wood door, forming a frightening O. This was followed by another and another—soon the entire door was alive with sharp teeth sawing away.

JD led the group effort of moving one of the kitchen's two refrigerators in front of the door. By the way the fridge shuddered with each renewed effort by the things on the other side of the door, he didn't think it would be much of a hindrance at all.

"Esto no está bien..." Luis whispered.

JD sized up their situation. There were seven of them

crammed into the postage-stamp-sized kitchen. Four men—Rowdy, Fisher, Luis, and himself—as well as two women, Trudy and Hailey, and a bawling little baby in the corner named Chester.

"We're doomed," Chester cried.

Doomed? Who the fuck says doomed in real life?

Ignoring the man, JD scanned the room.

No windows.

And the only other exit besides the door the suckers were determined to bite to bits was the hatch in the ceiling leading to the roof.

The bastard's right. We're doomed.

"Thanks a lot for leading those things right to us, by the way." Chester was pointing at him, red-faced. "If it wasn't for you—"

"Put a sock in it, will you, Chester?" Hailey said.

"I'm not talking to you, I'm talking to this redneck piece of—"

"Quiet," JD said.

"I will *not* be quiet! I have every right to—"

"Cierra la boca de una vez," Luis hissed.

"Oh, another country heard from. Speak English, amigo. Here in America we—"

"Shut up and listen," JD whispered intently, pointing up at the ceiling.

Everyone shut up; everyone listened.

Distinct from the sound of the suckers chewing through the door was the *thump-thump* of something on the roof.

JD fought back a scream as the hatch slowly began to open.

SEVENTEEN

The hatch to the roof had been JD's backup. But now, that was no longer an option. One of the thirsty things had smarts enough to climb its way atop the Dockside. Once it made its way inside the kitchen, it would have its pick of the litter.

JD wondered whose twisted and deformed face would appear above him. Would it be Woof, who'd had his innards scattered across all of Christendom? Or would it be poor Weena, her face mangled from Bo's deep kiss? Maybe the face would be unfamiliar—that of some hiker or passerby—teeth sprouting from its ears and nostrils, anywhere that teeth had no business being.

He didn't want to find out.

"Incoming!" he shouted, pointing up at the hatch.

It was Luis who jumped into action first. The cook scrambled up the ladder and grabbed hold of the hatch's handle. Whatever was above squealed angrily as the little door slammed shut. Luis held firm, slipping a foot beneath one of the ladder's metal rungs for support.

SUCKERVILLE

How long could the guy hold on? God only knew.

"Guess the boat's out," Fisher said, pulling a cigarette and lighting up.

"Would you mind?" Chester snarled, waving smoke out of his face.

Fisher snorted. "We're about to be eaten alive, and you're worried about your health?"

Hailey stopped the argument short by grabbing the cigarette out of Fisher's mouth and stubbing it out on the wall. "You may have given up, but I'm not done using my lungs. Now...what are we going to do?"

She turned to JD. So did Trudy. Hell, they were *all* looking at him. When did he become the leader of this little troop?

"Well," he said, "we know they're attracted to sounds. All we gotta do is—"

"I got this," Chester said, taking over. Even in this dire situation, the sonofabitch just *had* to be the boss. He dug out his phone and scrolled through his contacts. "When I booked this joint, Doc gave me the number. Fucking landline, do you believe it? I ring the phone out there, those things go after it, and we make a run for the boat."

"Listen..." JD said.

"It's ringing! Get ready."

Everyone went silent. The only noise was the sound of teeth gnawing away at the kitchen door.

"I don't hear any phone," Trudy whispered.

"I swear to God, it should be ringing." Chester stared at his screen.

Rowdy caught JD's eye, and the man suddenly realized what JD already knew.

"Hang up," Rowdy said, rubbing his face.

123

"No, I swear—"

"There's no phone."

Chester stared at Rowdy like he was from Mars. "The hell, you say?"

Rowdy gestured toward JD. "Our boy took it out with a Louisville Slugger."

"¡Mierda!" Luis groaned.

Chester took a menacing step toward JD.

JD raised his bat.

"I suck at sports, Chester, but I'm betting I could knock that head of yours clean outta the park if you take one more step toward me."

"JD..." Trudy said.

"Oh, big man!" Chester spat. "Put that down and we'll see how strong you are."

"Stop it, Chester."

"Helluva lot stronger than that rat piss you call beer."

"I'm warning you—"

Trudy grabbed the bat out of JD's hands and swung it hard at a stack of produce boxes. Tomatoes and jalapeños went flying.

"Put your dicks away, both of you, and let's figure out how to get out of here!"

JD eased back from Chester, but the tension in the room was as thick as molasses. Old Chester had it coming, but Trudy was right—now was not the time.

"Anybody got their keys on 'em?"

Everyone stared at Rowdy, wondering where he was going with this.

"Keys, people! Car keys."

JD had left the keys to Rowdy's truck...well, in the truck.

Fisher came up with the keys to his old clunker, but Rowdy waved them away.

"New car, new key. Anyone?"

Chester produced a fob from his pocket. "I got a 2023 Ram in pristine condition." Jesus, the guy couldn't say a single word without being a douche.

Rowdy swiped the fob without asking permission and gave it the once over. "It out front?"

JD knew that it was. He also knew that it had sustained massive damage to its caboose when he slammed into it, but he wasn't about to get things started again with Chester. Who knew what Trudy would do with that bat.

"It is."

The fridge in front of the door jerked, causing everyone in the room to flinch. All save for Luis, whose every ounce of strength was in great demand.

"Dependin' on its range, I'm thinkin' we set off your car alarm. They go for the truck, and we make a run for it."

Chester threw JD a smirking smile. It was the bastard's way of saying, "See? I'm gonna be the one to save us after all."

Fisher was peering into the space between the fridge and the door. "I hate to break it to you, but I don't think some of the things outside this door could skedaddle if they wanted to. They've pounded their teeth through this door like nails."

Rowdy looked at Hailey. "You're a strong girl, ain't you? Sorry, old habits...strong *woman*, right? Like, you work out and everything?"

Hailey eyed him warily. "I know my way around a gym, yeah."

Rowdy placed his hand on the outside kitchen wall. "This

bar ain't more than a glorified shed. With those killer gams of yours, I'm bettin' you could kick your way clean through this wall and not break a sweat."

Hailey cracked her knuckles. "I'm betting you're right."

"We're gonna have to move fast once we put this thing in motion. Once we're out, we go straight for the dock. We pile in, Fisher gets the boat started, and it's downriver as far as we can git. Sound good?"

Everyone agreed—it sounded damn good to them.

JD breathed a sigh of relief. Not only was Rowdy taking the pressure off him by taking the lead, but now they had a plan. And a darned good one at that.

He was about to compliment his buddy on his quick thinking when all the lights in the kitchen went out, plunging them into darkness.

No one screamed. No one dared. Everyone stood dead still, shocked into immobility.

JD felt terror creeping up his throat, but he swallowed it down. There was no use panicking. Panic now, and he was done for.

It was Rowdy, good old Rowdy, who broke the silence. "Nothin's changed. We're still a go. How 'bout you give us a little light from that phone of yours, Chester?"

JD heard Chester mumble under his breath, followed by the sound of something clattering to the floor.

"Did you just drop your phone?" JD asked incredulously.

"My hands are sweaty," Chester snapped.

"Here, lemme—"

"Back off!"

A sickening crunch of glass announced to the room that all was not well with Chester's phone.

"Shit!" A dim, flickering light illuminated the floor and everyone's feet as Chester tried to coax the device back to life. It was no use—the phone was DOA.

"Forget it. We're going. Honey—"

"Hailey."

"Get in position."

"I will if this blubbering idiot will get out of my way."

Chester sucked air as Hailey gave him a swift kick.

"Once she breaks through, we can't bottleneck, you hear? Gals first, then Fisher—"

"What about—?"

"You next, Chester. JD, then me, then Luis."

"Genial, el mexicano va ultimo," Luis groaned.

"Ready?"

JD heard the sound of a button clicking. But that was all. No alarm.

"Try it again," Fisher said.

"I am," Rowdy replied, his voice sharp. *Click-click, click-click.*

"It's too far away," Trudy said.

JD felt a hand brush his. He grasped it and gave a squeeze.

"It's going to be okay."

"Thanks," Fisher said back. "Now, let go of my hand."

"¡Dámela!"

JD caught the man's meaning. "Give the key to Luis!"

"Huh?" Rowdy said. "Ow! Whoever's elbow that is, get it out of my ribs."

"Sorry," Trudy said.

"Luis has a better shot being higher up. Pass him the key!"

JD listened as folks moved the key along from one to another.

Finally, Luis said, "La tengo."

JD heard the click followed by a single, electronic bleat.

"That's the lock, you moron."

"Shut up, Chester!" half the room said.

"He's got signal!" JD said. "Try another button."

Another click, and this time...

The Ram out in the parking lot squealed in angry outrage, convinced it was being stolen. A choir of screams answered, and soon the world was alive with the thundering footsteps of suckers eager for the kill.

"Honey!" Rowdy urged.

"Hailey!" the woman said as she kicked with all her might.

Either her might was pretty good or the Dockside's construction was very bad. In any case, it only took one strike to tear a hole in the drywall.

"¡Vámonos!" Luis cried.

Vámonos was fucking right, JD thought, as Hailey scurried through the hole.

EIGHTEEN

Concentrate on something else.

That's what Doc had said just before he stitched up JD's torn earlobe. It was what he had to do now—the prospect of crawling through that hole and exposing himself to possible death by sucker had frozen him in place.

"Concentrate on something else," he whispered to himself, taking the old vet's words to heart.

His thoughts landed on Trudy and Oquawka High's 2011 Prom. Details of that evening rose to the surface like dead fish. Trudy had been beautiful; he'd been wasted. Having forgotten her corsage at home, he tried to make light of it by offering her a bunch of dandelions instead. And, if that wasn't enough, he'd puked not once but twice during their ride to the VFW hall.

In between slow dances, Howie Miller had told him about the mini-bar Big Joe was setting up in the boy's locker room—Joe's dad was an assistant coach, and Joe had swiped his keys. He could have stayed on the dancefloor with Trudy, but his pickled brain wanted more booze.

What a fucking jerk. Why'd she even go with me in the first place?

"Speers! You're up!" Rowdy said.

The time for daydreaming was over. The nightmare awaited.

JD approached the opening Hailey had provided, courtesy of those massive leg muscles of hers. His heart was beating like a nervous bird in his chest. The light coming from the hole was dim, thanks to the cloud cover and the fact that some smart sucker had bitten into the power supply.

I hope it fried, JD thought.

"Git!" Rowdy gave him a kick in the rear, and the next thing he knew, he was tumbling into the grass.

JD braced himself, but there was no sucker welcoming committee awaiting him. From the sound of their distant shrieks, they were all over at Chester's Ram trying to get to the source of the screaming alarm.

Not so pristine anymore, motherfucker.

He picked himself up and scurried toward the dock as fast as his throbbing ankle would allow. Trudy and Hailey sat ready in the jon boat while Fisher hovered over the motor. Chester still stood on the dock, seemingly wary of the gap between dock and boat.

"Hop on in, Chester," JD said as he approached the tentative man. "Women and children first."

"Ha ha," Chester snarled. He sat on the dock and cautiously scooted himself into the boat on his rump, managing to send the craft rocking nonetheless. "Let's go."

"I'm not pulling this cord until everyone's present and accounted for," Fisher said.

"Present," Rowdy called out as he hit the gangplank.

"Where's Luis?" JD asked.

"He was right behind me."

"Well, he's not now."

"Maybe he decided to let the stupid gringos get themselves killed, who knows. We can't wait. Let's go!"

JD and Rowdy hopped aboard the boat. Six people in a fourteen-footer was a stretch—add Rowdy's considerable girth to the equation, and their endeavor became even more suspect.

"Riding a little low, folks," Fisher said as water lapped up over the starboard side.

"I'll stock up on Lean Cuisine tomorrow," Rowdy said. "Now, can we get this show on the road?"

Fisher turned back to the motor and gave the cord a yank. JD thought that if this had been a movie, the engine would have coughed and died, but the outboard dutifully came to life. Time to put some distance between them and the horde.

As they undid the moorings and cast off, a sound caught JD's attention. He looked back and spotted Dubya running their way, barking his fool head off.

The last time he'd seen the dog, it was chasing after its headless owner. This *was* Doc's boat after all—the fact the dog was racing toward them didn't necessarily mean...

Something burst from the water directly behind the boat, and JD didn't need to see the Hawaiian shirt to know it was Doc. Or least what was left of him.

Fisher let out a yelp and fell back, still gripping the control. The spinning propeller rose up, sending a spray of water shooting into the air.

Sucker-Doc grabbed hold of the propeller and bit down

with its new neck-mouth. The motor whined and flesh flew. Teeth went flying in every direction, like poison darts.

The sucker went limp, and yet its hands held tight to the motor, dragging down the boat's stern. Water poured in, swamping the craft.

Chester was the first to abandon ship. The Huckleberries were close behind. JD dove into the muddy water and quickly swam to the dock and hoisted himself out.

He helped the women out of the water, then held out his hand to Chester.

"I don't need your help," Chester said, struggling to get up onto the dock.

Figures.

JD looked back at the boat. Rowdy sat paralyzed at the bow. He was staring at Fisher.

"Damn," Fisher said as he reached back and yanked something out of his scalp.

A tooth.

"Get outta there, Rowdy!" JD called.

"I can't swim!" Rowdy cried back.

"You better fucking learn quick!"

Fisher's entire body spasmed. He coughed up blood. Awful wet noises came from his mouth, and JD could only imagine what mayhem the venom was inflicting on the man's insides. Suddenly, a single tooth speared his forehead, turning Fisher into a grotesque unicorn.

"Rowdy!"

Rowdy jumped ship. He went under, then bobbed to the surface. He worked his arms and legs in a poor man's dog paddle, managing to propel himself forward.

Fisher dove in after Rowdy. His progress through the water was much faster than his prey.

JD knelt and reached out a hand. Rowdy was just a few feet away. Four...three...two...

A dark blur passed by JD's periphery. A second later, Dubya landed in the jon boat. For everyone else, it was time to cut and run; for Dubya, it was time for a ride. Propelled by the impact of the dog's landing, the boat veered out into the current. It wasn't long before it was heading out into the river, the old dog barking his head off at its helm.

Fisher turned at the sound of the receding dog and switched targets. He spun in the water and shot off after Dubya like the world's hungriest narwhale.

Rowdy rammed one of the dock's pilings with his head and grunted. JD and Hailey hoisted him out. The effort caused JD's ankle to sing like the dickens.

"What now?" Chester asked. His tone suggested he was accusing everyone in the group for the pickle he now found himself in.

"What now?" Rowdy spluttered, coughing up half of the Mississippi in the process. "We're screwed, that's what now."

They were five, now—five soaked and frightened people. And they were incredibly exposed.

"Back to the bar?" Rowdy suggested.

"No way. I say we split up," Chester blurted. "They can't get us all if we split up."

"Hush," JD said.

"Suits me," Hailey said.

"We're not splitting up," Trudy pushed back.

"Luis had the right fucking idea," Rowdy said.

JD waved his hands, hushing the bickering group. "Will you all pipe down and listen!"

Everyone went quiet.

"I don't hear anything," Chester growled.

"And that," JD whispered, "is my fucking point."

The Ram's alarm had gone silent.

"Well, that's that," Rowdy moaned. "Been nice knowin' y'all."

The silence was replaced by the musical blare of a car horn.

"Is that...?" JD asked

Everyone nodded. It was. The car horn was playing "La Cucaracha."

JD heard the revving of a souped-up engine followed by the squeals of hungry suckers. He limped down the gangplank and hugged the tavern wall. Slowly he inched to the corner and peeked around.

Luis's turquoise VW was making donuts in the parking lot, kicking up sand. The swarm of suckers was racing to keep up. Luis spun his car around again and again, clocking as many as he could.

Then, with a final flourish of trumpets, the cook took off into the night, pursued by the frothing horde.

Whether the guy was trying to play Pied Piper to the suckers or just trying to save his own hide, JD didn't care. Luis's loud departure offered a window of opportunity.

"Let's go!" he called back to the group.

"Go where?" Rowdy asked.

JD gave him a wink. "To the Airstream."

The group made a beeline for the camper.

If smashing into the back of Chester's Ram with Rowdy's

pickup hadn't done the vehicle in, the suckers certainly had. In their frenzy to get to the alarm, they had ripped up its pristine exterior. It looked like it had been attacked by an army of giant can openers.

"My truck!" Chester cried.

"Hope it's under warranty," JD said.

He hobbled over to Rowdy's pickup and yanked the deflated airbags out of the cab. "She's never gonna win any beauty contests, but I think she'll run."

Rowdy grabbed the Airstream's door handle. It didn't budge.

"Fuckin' Kate," he growled.

Hailey came up behind him. "I got this."

She grabbed the handle and twisted. Both she and the metal groaned. There was a click, and the door swung open.

"Everybody, inside," JD urged. "Let's go, let's go!"

Chester ducked in first, elbowing past Hailey.

"You're welcome," Hailey said.

"Think this beauty can hold up against them things?" Rowdy asked.

"It made it through Hurricane Tate when I was down in Florida. A few scrapes is all. She'll hold up."

"I hope so," Rowdy said. "Otherwise we're nothin' but tasty treats inside a fancy wrapper. Which road you takin'?"

"I figured the best route would be—"

Someone laughed inside the camper. Another chortle burst forth, followed by a guffaw. Soon, the Airstream was rocking with laughter.

"What the...?" Rowdy said.

JD followed his buddy inside. The Huckleberries were doubled over, shaking with fits of laughter.

Scattered about the floor were a couple of dozen battered, metal canisters hissing like snakes. Others remained in their storage rack, which lay catawampus against the wall.

Rowdy picked up one of the whistling tanks.

"Looks like your ex has been breakin' bad. Nitrous oxide. Perk of being a dental hygienist, I guess. She must get a pretty penny for these on the street." Rowdy snorted. "Pretty penny...pretty penny..." Soon, he was laughing along with the rest of them.

"We gotta...we gotta..." The gas-induced laughter was infectious. JD thought his diaphragm would bust. They had to get on the road, but...but...

Trudy leaned against JD, laughing her head off. "If we don't get...hee...if we don't get going...hee!"

"I know! Ha! I know," JD barked. "We're dead!"

"As doornails!" Trudy snorted.

This doubled them both over, JD draped across Trudy's back.

Some small part of JD's brain still as yet unaffected by the laughing gas urged him on, and he crawled toward the door. The rest of the group were in the throes of unwanted hysterics, all save for Chester, who stumbled about the Airstream, dizzy and disoriented.

"Stop that!" he yelled at no one in particular.

JD found the door, fumbled for the latch, and tumbled outside.

"Freeze!"

JD looked up to find himself staring down the business end of a Glock.

The owner of the weapon shined a brilliant light in his

eyes, blinding him. Rowdy was wrong when he said the cavalry wasn't coming. In fact, they were already here.

"Speers? That you?"

Holy fucking shitballs...

Cal the Cop lowered his flashlight and sneered down at him.

"Looky what we've got here, hon."

"Who you calling hon?" JD snapped back.

A figure stepped out of the shadows, and put her hand on Cal's shoulder.

"Me, that's who," Kate said. "Get your gun off my ex, Cal, or I might be tempted to have you pull the trigger."

NINETEEN

"Watch your head."

JD ducked, but Cal guided his forehead into the SUV's doorframe.

"Damn. Sorry about that, JD."

The cuffs bit into JD's wrists as he squirmed into the back seat of the Interceptor.

"You don't know what you're doing, you idiot!"

"You're going to want to tame that mouth of yours. I am *not* in the mood. Capt. Mikita's riding my ass about prank calls coming from the Dockside, my lady's up in arms about a stolen camper, and I've got two units who've gone AWOL. Do you *really* want to test me tonight?"

"Please, Cal. Please!"

Cal slammed the door closed, trapping JD in the Interceptor's back seat.

A second later, Kate opened the rear hatch and set a case of Huckleberry Beer in the trunk space, followed by two large black duffels. JD recognized them as the bags he'd carried for Trudy and Hailey—heavy as hell and definitely *not* Kate's.

JD pressed up against the metal grate that separated him from his ex.

"Kate, you gotta listen to me—"

"No, I don't."

"We're all in danger."

"No, JD. Just you."

He tried a different tack. "I don't give a shit about what you've got in the camper—"

"Oh, but you will." There was fire in her eyes. "See, after Cal tracked down my stolen Airstream, he found the nitrous you stole from Dr. Hemming's office."

"What? I never—"

She patted the bag sitting atop the case of beer next to him.

"And when he caught up with you, he found even more stolen goods in your possession."

Cal leaned in behind Kate. "Now should that beer find its way into my fridge instead of evidence...well, c'est la vie."

Cal kissed Kate hard.

She giggled. "You're bad!"

"No, *you're* bad."

My God...the two were made for each other.

Something caught Cal's attention—JD could see the quick shift in the man's demeanor. He turned to see what Cal was looking at.

The Airstream was a-rockin'.

Cal's weapon was back out.

"Who's with you?"

"Nobody," he lied, more by instinct than anything. "I mean—"

The door to the camper creaked open, and Trudy braced

herself in the doorway. In her little outfit and laughing like a fool, she looked like an extra from *Hee Haw*.

"Cal! Don't shoot!" JD cried, straining against his cuffs. "She's with me, *she's with me!*"

"Chester threw up!" Trudy hooted.

Kate stared at JD and shook her head. "Wow. Just, wow."

A branch snapped nearby.

Someone was coming out of the woods.

Cal shined his light in the direction of the sound.

"Show yourself!"

A man in blue shuffled out of the shadows. His eyes were pale, and the light glinted off the shield on his chest.

"Ritter? Is that you?" Cal called, dropping his guard. "Jesus Christ, don't sneak up on a man like that. You want to tell me why you turned off your radio?"

JD's guard, on the other hand, was up—way up. The approaching officer's hands were as large as catcher's mitts. And they were covered in...

Teeth.

Shit. Shit, shit, shit, shit, shit.

JD pounded his head against the glass. "Cal, look out! *Look out!*"

The cop, formerly known as Ritter, snarled. The sucker spread its arms wide, its hand-mouths open and ready for business. It crouched low, and then...it sprang.

As fate would have it, it wasn't Cal who needed to look out—it was Kate.

Ritter landed on top of her, knocking the wind out of her and toppling her to the ground. From his vantage point, JD couldn't see what was happening to his ex, and he was glad of that. The wet ripping sounds were more than enough to paint a picture.

Cal must have seen the whole thing up close and in Technicolor. He fired his Glock, the report echoing through the night.

Suddenly, the night was filled with movement. The Dockside's loyal patrons, their bodies defiled by toothy deformity, poured from the woods, screaming their way toward the Interceptor.

Either Luis got away or he'll be showing up soon, sucker mouth and all...

Cal meanwhile dropped all semblance of authority. He hustled into the SUV and revved the engine.

"What do you think you're doing?" JD screamed.

Cal didn't answer, just threw the Interceptor in reverse and swung it around for a quick getaway. In so doing, the headlights caught Officer Ritter hunkered over Kate, who was fighting a rapidly losing battle. Her green scrubs were drenched in blood.

Cal floored it, and the SUV kicked up sand. JD desperately tried to spot Trudy. She had to get back in the Airstream, he had to warn her...

But a minute later, the Dockside was retreating in the distance, and the open road lay ahead.

JD raged in the backseat. If it wasn't for the plexiglass separating them, he would have climbed into the front and throttled Cal, cuffs or no cuffs.

"You coward! You fucking coward!" he shouted, kicking at the partition. Tears spilled down JD's face. He'd loved Kate once upon on a time, and those kind of feelings never go away. Not completely. When Ritter bit into her, it was all he could do to keep from breaking.

Cal didn't say a word. He didn't call for backup. Instead, he hit the country road going ninety and only sped up from there.

JD had failed them all.

Trudy.

Hailey, Rowdy.

Hell, even that dickhead, Chester.

The suckers were going to tear the Airstream open, and that would be the end of them.

And the weasel behind the wheel had just turned tail and run. JD could practically feel Cal sweating into his shorts.

"What kind of cop are you?"

"Shut up."

"What kind of *man* are you?"

"I'm warning you."

"If I weren't in these cuffs—"

The rear windshield shattered with a deafening *crack*.

At first, JD thought Cal had hauled off and taken a shot at him, but the man had both hands on the wheel. Plus, when the cop whipped his head around, he looked as confused as JD did.

"What'd you do?" Cal shouted.

"Nothing!"

Something crawled in through the window and landed in the back. The only thing separating it from JD was a wire partition. Things were about to get ugly. After seeing what those creatures did to Chester's Ram, a single metal grate wasn't going to stop them.

The thing hissed, low and throaty. JD still couldn't see it, but he twisted around, setting his back against the plexiglass partition and readying to do battle with his feet. If the thing got through the grate, that battle would be short-lived.

The pale thing raised itself up and dug its fingers into the wire mesh. And when it bit down on the metal, JD realized he had run out of road.

He also realized he *knew* who the sucker was. The badly-tattooed dice on its shoulder were a dead giveaway.

Jesus, it's Virgil Orr.

The man had been a regular down at Guppy's Lanes with a 220 bowling average. Now he was tearing his way through steel to get his teeth into JD. Funny how life works out sometimes.

The sucker tore free chunks of the metal partition as if it were made of cardboard, ignoring its torn and bleeding gums in its frenzy to get inside. JD felt like a man in a shark cage—one that was being ripped to shreds.

"If only there was a cop around when you needed 'em!" JD spat.

Cal was no help whatsoever. The man had checked out. Virgil Orr was crawling through the grate toward him, and Cal was—

The plexiglass partition slid open. Gunfire erupted inside the vehicle, and JD's hearing went running for the hills. He felt the concussive blasts as Cal fired again and again, and sucked in the firecracker scent of the powder. But if Cal had said anything—like *get your head down* or *cover your ears*—he hadn't hear it.

The bullets struck Virgil square in the forehead, splitting the top of his head in two. Another few shots and gray matter decorated the ceiling.

The sucker gave one last fitful grab at JD, and Cal fired until he was out of ammo.

JD flipped back around.

"Took you long enough!" he shouted, the bells of Notre Dame ringing in his ears.

Cal was staring back at him, weapon in hand, a look of disbelief on his face.

"Watch the road!" JD screamed.

Cal turned back front, but it was too late. The SUV swerved out of control, careening off the road and down a steep embankment. Below, a boggy inlet lay waiting. Cal tried to brake, but gravity was in charge now.

The Interceptor hit the water. JD smashed into the seat in front of him, and he felt his nose snap. Warm blood gushed down his chin.

Is this how it ends? JD wondered as the SUV slowly slipped into the swampy waters.

Apparently, it was.

TWENTY

"Is this how it ends for you, JD?"

Vice Principal Howard had his hands folded on top of a thick folder—within, every bit of paperwork documenting every misdeed in JD's colorful high school career.

The VP patted the folder.

"It doesn't have to be, you know. You can write another chapter of your story if you want. One that doesn't end in your leaving this school without a diploma. Maybe we should examine what that story might be like."

JD's father snorted. He wondered if Mr. Howard could smell the Old Crow on the man's breath.

"Did I say something funny, Mr. Speers?"

"No, sir. It's just..."

"Just what?"

JD's father stuck a thumb at him. "I mean, look at the boy. He ain't never gonna graduate. It ain't in his blood. The sooner you kick him out, the sooner he gets a job. And *that*, sir, is how my son's story is gonna go."

Mr. Howard adjusted his glasses and pulled a pamphlet

from the desk drawer. "You know, there are tutoring programs—"

JD's father rose, albeit unsteadily. He waved off the pamphlet.

"Thanks anyway."

JD followed his father out of the office, head down. As soon as they were in the hallway, Roger Speers slapped his kid hard across the face.

"You make me come down here again, and you'll get worse."

JD fought back tears. "Sorry to keep you from your drinking buddies."

"Excuse me?"

"Nothing, Papa."

His father glared at him. "I thought not."

With that, Roger Speers weaved his way to the exit.

JD glanced around. He'd suddenly become the center of attention—clusters of students stood nearby, whispering to each other. By the end of the day, the whole school would know JD Speers's old man had smacked his son on school grounds.

"Fuck off," he snarled.

A few moments later, he was rummaging through his locker. He pulled out *War and Peace,* the largest book he'd found in the library. He surreptitiously paged through the tome and came to the spot where the pint of Yukon Jack lay nestled inside the cut-out pages.

He shielded himself with the locker door to take a shot, but a nasty laugh caught his attention. He peeked to his left and spied Jeff Renfro and his football buddies circled around a girl in fluorescent green leggings.

"Come on, don't be like that," Renfro sneered.

Jeff Renfro was six-two and more brawns than brains. There were rumors about what he might have done to Kelly Mannix the night of the game with Aledo. Kelly never came back to school, and Jeff had sat out two games. From the look of things, the guy hadn't learned his lesson.

"I'm late for class," the girl said, trying to break out of the circle. "I've got to go."

Jeff blocked her path. "Not before you give me an answer."

"You want an answer? How about *no,* how about *never,* how about *not in a million years!"*

The look on Jeff Renfro's face when she said that made JD snort. The girl sure had some grit.

Jeff turned. The guy was so angry, JD thought he might stroke out.

"What are you laughing at?"

JD sighed. The world was full of bullies: his father, the mouth-breather in the football jersey. Maybe it was the slap, maybe it was the look of fear on the girl's face. Whatever it was, he was past caring.

"You, you fucking rump roast." Not the best comeback, but it would do.

Oquawka High's defensive line moved on him as one. They lit into JD with abandon, and he laughed through the whole thing. Even as his jaw popped, even as his molar cracked, even as his lip split and blood filled his mouth. He kept laughing as they beat him to a pulp, until finally the punches ceased.

He must have been an unnerving sight, as the football bruisers slowly backed away.

"What's wrong with you?" Jeff said, his fists covered in JD's blood.

JD laughed on, spitting red.

The bell rang; the show was over. Students scurried to class, and Jeff and his buddies stalked off.

"That was a stupid thing to do."

JD looked up through his one good eye and saw the girl in the fluorescent leggings standing over him.

"Yeah, that's my speciality," he said, testing out his jaw. "What was his damage?"

"I wouldn't go to the prom with him. Guess his little ego couldn't take it."

She helped JD up. He was going to be sore for a while.

"Still, thanks for...whatever that was," she said. Was she grinning?

"I guess that means you gotta go to the prom with me, seeing as I rescued you."

Now she *was* grinning. "Rescued me? Look at yourself. You didn't rescue shit."

She turned and headed off down the hall.

"The name's Trudy, in case you were wondering," she called back.

JD gave a little wave. "Later, Trudy."

"Yes, by the way."

"Yes, what?"

She just kept on walking, a vision in bright green.

"Yes, what?" he cried.

Cold water hit JD's ankles, rousing him.

Cal moaned in the front seat.

"You gotta get me outta these cuffs, Cal," JD said, feeling the water reach his calves.

Cal glanced back at him. He sported massive black eyes despite, or perhaps due to, the airbag deploying. The vacant look in those eyes told JD that the cop was more than likely concussed.

"What's...what's...?" Cal mumbled.

Something in the water brushed JD's leg. He pulled up his legs and scrambled onto the seat.

"Come on, Cal, snap out of it!"

"What's that?" Cal said, finally finishing his thought.

JD froze as he spied what *that* was.

Pouring out of the Interceptor's air vents like black tears were scores of squirming leeches.

TWENTY-ONE

The leeches were a good five times larger than your average crop. They were fat, and in leechworld, fat meant well-fed. JD wondered *what* they'd been feeding on. Or who.

Cal shrieked, and it was not a pleasant sound. Filled with desperation, it set JD's teeth on edge.

"The keys, Cal. I need the goddamn keys."

The cop raised his hand. Three chubby leeches hung from his palm like dark appendages. JD could see them pulsing as they fed.

"The keys, Cal!"

Cal tried to shake the things loose, but it was no use—they would not be denied their feast. He tried his door, but it wouldn't budge. The driver's side was wedged tight against a sunken log.

In a feat of backseat gymnastics, JD leaned forward, twisted his left hand and followed through with his right as he raised and rotated his arms. The result was that his cuffed hands were now in front of him, although his shoulders would be screaming soon. It was a trick his father, no stranger to the back of cop cars, had taught him. Some fathers taught their sons how to play baseball; his taught him this.

He reached through the open partition and clapped Cal on the shoulder. "Keys!"

Cal had no interest in what JD had to say. He raised his other hand in front of his face—five more leeches were going to town, blood trickling down his arm from where the things had latched on.

The front of the cabin was filling up quicker than the back as the Interceptor settled into the water. Soon, Cal would be up to his waist in Mississippi muck, and the keys to the handcuffs—assuming he had them on his belt or in a pocket—would be beneath the surface.

JD reached down with both hands and felt around on Cal's utility belt. The intrusion broke the cop's fixation on his leech-covered hands.

"Back in the back and get face down!" Cal barked.

"Don't think you're in any position to give me orders, Cal."

JD worked his hands along the belt—pepper spray, a Leatherman tool, radio...but no keys yet.

Cal batted him away, splashing water as he did, for now, the water *had* reached his waist.

JD steeled himself and plunged his hands beneath the surface and picked up where he left off, finding a pen, an extra set of cuffs...and a small utility container. He ripped the flap open and snaked his fingers inside. Bingo.

The cop grabbed at him, but his muscles no longer

seemed to be his. He only managed to knock the keys out of JD's hands.

"Oh, come on!" JD cried.

Back into the water his hands went. His fingers danced along the leather seat until they located the keys. As he wrapped his hand around them, something snaked against his wrist.

JD drew back quickly, just in time to see the leech leap out of the water like an Asian carp—the damn thing actually leaped!

He had to forcibly steady himself in order to slip the key into the cuff. The lock released with a click.

"God, it hurts!" Cal cried.

The cop's sudden outburst startled JD, and the keys slipped from his fingers. No matter—his hands were free, despite the metal bracelet still hanging from his left wrist.

The SUV shifted, dropping a few feet deeper into the muck.

"Hold on. I'm going to get you out of here," JD swore.

"It hurts, it *hhh-uugh-ghhh!*"

Cal's head snapped to the side, his vertebrae suddenly betraying him. The look of shock on the cop's face needed no translation. The man's body went into full seizure mode, his arms and legs kicking up water, sending leeches flying. They stuck wherever they hit—the ceiling, the windows, and even...

Oh, my God.

Even Cal's tongue.

"Lnn-ahh-muh-muhh!"

The jumbo leech bit down, sucking with all the strength of an industrial vacuum. Cal's tongue swelled horribly, purple and bloated, and soon he was choking on it.

The guy was toast, and JD knew it. Whatever animosity he had against the man, he wouldn't wish Cal's fate on anyone.

Time to save himself.

JD turned to the rear partition. Virgil had chomped quite a hole in the grate, but it would still be a tight squeeze with sharp metal edges poised and ready to bite.

He took a deep breath and crawled through, arms first. As expected, the grate was eager to draw blood—metal dug into flesh as he wriggled through the small opening.

Sonofabitch!

He landed on Virgil's remains. The force of his landing caused the dead Virgil to exhale, and the noxious breath that gushed forth—all iron and algae and rot— almost knocked JD out.

He raised up, ready to extract himself from the SUV.

An earsplitting squeal filled the vehicle. JD knew he shouldn't look back. He should get the hell out of the SUV and keep on moving. But he *did* look back, and what he saw was the stuff of nightmares.

Cal was crawling from the front seat to the rear. The leeches had done their job, all right. The cop's face was nothing but mouths, with more bursting forth every second. Pink pus dripped down his chin.

Even his eyes are mouths.

Two ovals of pinprick teeth now sat where Cal's eyes used to be, like twin Venus flytraps eager for their meal.

The cop was moving fast. There was no way JD would get out in time.

He searched around, desperate to find a flare or a tire wrench, anything he could use to slow the newly-minted sucker.

What his hand landed upon was a bottle of beer.

The case of Huckleberry Sour Cal had pilfered had split open—beer bottles lay scattered about. It wasn't much, but it was something.

JD raised the bottle just in time to see Cal stick his head through the grate, all those mouths flexed and ready to get their teeth into him.

He brought the bottle down with a sickening *thunk.*

The bottle shattered with the force of the blow, and the familiar stench of Chester's sour concoction filled the air.

Cal stopped short.

As the beer ran down the sucker's face, something unexpected happened. One by one, the mouths began to close, puckering up to avoid sucking up the sour brew.

JD felt as if he'd been struck by lightning. He grabbed another bottle, and this time, instead of cracking it over Cal's head, he twisted the cap.

He suddenly understood what Doc had figured out before he lost his head, the reason the suckers had gone into hiding after he'd crashed Woof's bike into the jukebox.

Doc had stuck his hand in the jar of pickled eggs, after which the leeches hadn't latched on. He'd fired up the smoke eater to rid the tavern of the stench of spilled sour, and the suckers had played possum.

The bastards can't stomach vinegar.

Which meant they hated Chester's beer almost as much as he did.

JD upended the bottle and poured out its contents over Cal's head.

The result was instantaneous.

Cal's entire face puckered inward, mouths trying to escape Chester's poison. JD heard bones crack as the cop swallowed his own chin, cheeks, nose.

The sucker backed off, retreating to the front seat before ducking beneath the water.

The sucker's swift movements caused the Interceptor to resume its slide into the swamp. Water rushed in faster and faster. Soon, there would be nothing but the dark depths.

JD kicked into high gear. He frantically collected as many bottles as he could and tossed them through the rear window onto the shore. Then he grabbed the black duffel and chucked it out as well—if he was going to carry all that beer, he'd need something to tote it in.

JD launched himself through the shattered rear window. He hit the ground with a bounce and only just managed to keep from tumbling back into the water by grabbing hold of a clump of weeds.

The Interceptor groaned before slipping beneath the water's surface.

JD scrambled up the incline to join the beer bottles littering the shoulder. He took a mental inventory.

Twisted ankle: check; busted nose: check; deep cuts on his arms, head, and neck: check, check, check.

Still, things could be worse. He could be stuck inside the SUV currently sinking into the muddy depths of this inlet.

He gathered up the bottles and found he had eighteen in total. It would have to do. A plan was formulating, and although it seemed like a stretch, it was the only plan he had.

He had to save Trudy.

He quickly unzipped the duffel, eager to dump its contents and get the beer stashed so he could hustle back to the Dockside. JD pulled out half a dozen Huckleberry Beer T-shirts until he landed upon something that made his eyes go wide.

"God bless the Huckleberries."

TWENTY-TWO

The T-shirt canon was a Mach-9 Multi-Launch with a bright red barrel sporting the Huckleberry Beer motto: *Suck on this!*

It was one of the most beautiful things JD had ever seen. Whether or not the attached CO_2 tank gave the gun enough oomph to fire a twelve-ounce bottle of sour remained to be seen.

Guess I'll find out soon enough.

He only had a rough estimate as to how far they'd traveled in Cal's SUV. One thing he did know was that going back the same way, via the county road, would add at least an extra mile to the journey back. Best to stick close to the water.

He trudged on as quickly as he could. The way was muddy, and the wet, sucking ground did its best to slow him down, threatening to rob him of his shoes.

I think I know this inlet.

From where or when, he hadn't a clue. But he did have a

vague idea that if he followed it around, he'd come out of the woods just south of the tavern.

Something leaped from the water, startling him. JD whirled about. By the time he realized it was just a frog, he'd already fired. The beer bottle hurtled over the creature's head and plonked into the water.

He was down one Huckleberry Beer.

Seventeen bottles of beer on the wall...

JD reloaded and pressed on.

He tried not to think too far ahead. Right now, his mission was to get back to the Airstream. If he tried to think past that point, things got hazy fast, and his nerve wavered. Best not to think...at all. Just keep putting one foot in front of the other.

JD struck something embedded in the earth, and he teetered off balance. He tried catching himself but to no avail. He tumbled face-first into the muck.

Pulling himself to his feet, he glanced down. It appeared he had tripped over an old metal drum, now almost completely submerged in water. Beyond that drum lay another and yet another—a whole gaggle of them, corroded green paint setting them apart from the rest of the swampy hues.

JD took a closer look. What he had at first thought was algae clinging to the drum's surface was, in fact, something else altogether. Swaths of writhing leeches hung onto its sides. And were they...feeding?

He stumbled backward, not just in reaction to the squirming beasties, but because a terrible realization washed over him.

A few months ago, his bank account had been as empty

as a church on Tuesday—in fact, it was in negative territory. Try as he might, he couldn't rustle together enough cash to right the ship.

After a few failed attempts at hustling pool—could it really be called hustling when the hustler was a piss-poor pool player?—JD had turned to Rowdy for help.

"I ain't givin' you no loan 'cause we both know how that's gonna end," his buddy had said. "But I *will* hook you up with a way to earn you some cheddar."

Rowdy was as good as his word, and the next day, he introduced JD to Jerry Jensen.

"Need you to help me haul some shit."

"What kind of shit?"

"Whadda you care?"

As it turned out, the *shit* was a dozen drums from the old agricultural college up in Keithsburg that shut down in the seventies. They met the property's new owner at the site, and Jerry had assured the man the load would be going to the waste disposal facility in Naperville, three hours away.

The drums were bright green and plastered with government warning labels. When JD had asked Jerry how dangerous he thought the stuff was, the man replied, "Well, it ain't sody pop."

Instead of hitting the highway, Jerry had insisted they stop in at Stiffy's for a quick nip. After that, a second at Muhlberg's and a third, fourth, and fifth at Doc's. By the time the two of them had gotten back to the truck, JD's head was swimming like a Busby Berkeley musical.

"Let's do it tomorrow, eh?" JD slurred. "I gotta crash."

"Bail now, and I ain't payin' you one dime."

JD had bailed, poorer for the day on account of all the rounds he'd bought.

He stared down at the drum graveyard. The load hadn't made it to Naperville—in fact, it hadn't even made it out of town. Jerry Jensen had cut corners, and here they sat. Rusting and oozing their poison into the water.

His original assessment of the man was correct: Jerry Jensen was an asshole.

JD pulled a beer from the bag and twisted off the cap. He poured out a bit for his fallen friends and then flung the bottle as hard as he could. It hit the drum dead on, spilling foaming beer across its surface. As the liquid came in contact with the leeches, they let go as if suddenly electrified, dropping into the water in droves.

If he ever saw Chester again, he owed the bastard a beer. Not one of these undrinkable sours, of course, but a nice, cold...

An eruption of bubbles broke the surface of the water.

Something was moving toward him.

JD quickly reloaded the canon as the bubbles moved toward the shore.

The pale woman who emerged from the water had once been a looker, no question about that, but that was before the suckers had lit into her, made her one of their own.

The first thing he noticed about her was that she had mouths where her breasts should be. Her skin was white and wrinkled from her time beneath the water. She wasn't wearing a stitch of clothes, which made her appearance all that much more unnerving.

The stink of spoiled meat preceded her, and JD wondered how many people she'd drained.

I'm not going to be one of them.

JD readied the canon, but his hands were wet with beer, and he almost lost his grip. He caught the gun, but the preloaded beer unceremoniously dropped out of the barrel and rolled down the incline and into the water.

He was a gunslinger with an empty shooting iron.

The pale woman pressed forward. JD drew back, stumbling over his own feet. Not looking where he was going, he caught an outcropping of rock with his heel and twisted his ankle yet again. This time, white heat raced up his calf, and he couldn't stifle the scream that burst from his mouth.

The pale woman screamed back with all her mouths in a harmony of hatred and hunger.

JD scooted up the hill on his ass, not daring to let the sucker out of his sight.

The sucker, for her part, paused at the water's edge and crouched. She stuck her hands in the dark water and brought them back up a moment later, covered in squirming leeches. She plucked one free and held it up in front of her face.

And then...she flung it at him.

The leech whizzed past his head and struck a downed branch next to him—it stuck like a dart.

The pale woman plucked another leech free and another, unleashing a barrage of fleshy projectiles. JD dodged them as best he could.

When the pale woman paused, JD thought he might, just *might,* have a chance to reload. But the sucker was faster than him. She bounded out of the water and up the hill, ready to chow down like it was going out of style.

JD raised the empty canon in a futile gesture and looked

away. The thing was close and getting closer. Soon, it was right on top of him.

Whether or not the sucker was aiming for the Mach-9 Multi-Launch, when it landed atop JD, it clamped down on the barrel with its jaws.

JD pulled the trigger.

A shot of compressed air blasted a hole in the back of the sucker's rotting head, chunks of meat and bone showering the shore.

That's for Doc.

The thing's eyes flickered once, and it flopped to the side.

JD rose quickly, but there was no need. The pale woman was still and very, *very* dead.

Before he packed up his gear and continued on his way, JD removed his flannel shirt and placed it over the corpse. The suckers had robbed her of her dignity, defiling her body with their poison. Giving the poor woman back a bit of her modesty was the least he could do.

The bag grew heavier with every step, and his body wanted to give out, but he pushed on. And when he finally came upon the clearing that led to the Dockside, he felt no small measure of relief.

The feeling was short-lived.

In the distance, he could see the Airstream. And it was crawling with suckers.

TWENTY-THREE

As JD surveyed the scene, a song popped into his head, as was typical of key moments in his life. When he first laid eyes on Kate, he couldn't get "I Feel Like a Woman" out of his mind; when she filed for divorce, he carried around "Folsom Prison Blues" for weeks. There was no rhyme or reason to these earworms, and if they had any greater message for him, any wisdom to impart, he never deciphered it. And so when Led Zeppelin's "Kashmir" kicked in, he rolled with it. Apparently, his death would have a soundtrack.

Suckers clung to the metal camper like lampreys on a whale. They undulated as they chewed, casting the scene in a morbidly orgiastic light.

Whether the sounds JD heard as he approached were nitrous-induced laughter or screams of terror was anybody's guess. If he didn't move fast, it would be nothing but screams soon enough.

JD hunkered down at the edge of the clearing. He grabbed a brew and doused himself as liberally as a teenager applying cologne, hoping it would add at least a modicum of protection.

He figured he might be able to get off three shots before the horde attacked. Once he had their undivided attention, he'd have about a dozen Huckleberry Beers left for his last stand. That should allow the folks trapped in the Airstream time enough to make their escape. At least, he hoped it would.

He reloaded the canon. Then, he filled his pockets, back and front, with beer bottles and stuck as many as he could inside his waistband until he resembled the world's most ambitious shoplifter. It wasn't the most comfortable arrangement, but he had bigger things to worry about.

Like what he was going to do once he ran out of beer.

Everything's going to be okay.

And with that lie in mind, he began his approach.

He could hear them now, the slavering creatures, grinding away at the camper's metal shell, hissing in antici-pation of the feast within.

JD said a mental sayonara and fired. The canon let out a *whumpf* and the first Huckleberry Beer sailed high in the air.

Despite proving that the Mach-9 Multi-Launch wasn't actually limited to firing T-shirts, JD's heart sank as the beer landed well shy of its target.

Damn!

He'd have to move closer. And that meant he'd probably only get off two shots before they turned on him. Two...maybe one.

JD scrambled forward, bottles toasting each other in his waistband. Once he judged he was close enough, he stuffed another bottle down the barrel and fired again.

This time, the range was good, but instead of striking the Airstream's metal siding, the beer glanced off a sucker hanging off the side. The thing shook off the blow and dug its teeth even deeper into the camper's side.

"Sonofabitch," JD cursed under his breath and moved closer still.

He extracted a bottle from his waistband and gave it a kiss for good measure before loading it into the chamber.

A section of the Airstream's roof buckled with a groan, its structure compromised by the massive amount of metal torn free by the suckers. When it collapsed completely, the creatures would pour into the camper—Trudy, Rowdy, and the others would be torn to bits in mere seconds.

A scream broke through the chaos, and JD knew at once it was Trudy. The suckers were on the verge of getting inside.

With the rock anthem pounding in his head, he raised the T-shirt canon and took aim at the riveted metal siding.

"Time to get the Led out," he said, and pulled the trigger.

The bottle shot forward, striking the camper dead on. The glass shattered, christening the Airstream in Huckleberry Sour.

The suckers nearest the impact point got doused soundly. At first, JD thought his efforts were a bust, but then the first creature detached, followed by another.

Instead of turning on him, the two fell to the ground, writhing and clawing at their throats.

JD quickly reloaded and fired without thinking. The second bottle had a similar effect—three more of the things dropped off the Airstream, squealing in pain.

A man with a mouth the size of a garbage can lid rose

atop the camper. It aimed its gaping maw in his direction and loosed a gurgling roar.

That was that. He had their attention now. Time to fall back.

"Rowdy!" JD cried, stumbling backward, "I'll draw them off. When I do, get everyone outta here!"

He could have sworn someone shouted a reply, but it was drowned out by the suckers. They were dropping off the Airstream in droves.

JD fired as he retreated, picking off creatures one by one. The beer was no silver bullet, but it definitely slowed the things down; however, the more Huckleberry ammo he fired, the less distance he got. The tank was running out of CO^2.

One nimble monstrosity—a hiker before her untimely transformation—broke from the crowd, galloping toward him on all fours. The thing's mouth opened wider and wider the closer it got, its thicket of teeth poised to run him through.

He pulled a bottle from his rear pocket and raised it as the music swelled in his head.

"Bring it!" he shouted.

The nimble sucker didn't bring it. In fact, it stopped dead in its tracks. Something else had grabbed its attention. The sucker's curiosity was infectious—soon, the entire horde had called off the chase.

That's when JD spotted the white Ram, all hickeyed up by its previous encounter with the suckers, rocking back and forth, trying to extract itself from Rowdy's pickup.

JD's friends had gotten themselves out of the Airstream and smack dab into trouble. He'd drawn the monsters away from the camper, but now, his draw wasn't draw enough. The revving Ram was just too tasty to pass up.

"Damn it!" JD cried in vain as the suckers rushed Chester's truck.

TWENTY-FOUR

For a moment, it looked like Chester and company were about to get away, scot-free. Chester had managed to tear the Ram loose, albeit not without dealing Rowdy's ancient pickup a deathblow in the process—in the battle between old school and new school, new had won by a mile.

But Chester hesitated a few seconds after he was in the clear. Whether it was surprise that he'd actually accomplished the feat or indecision as to what to do next, it didn't matter. Those extra seconds proved costly.

The horde swarmed the Ram, beating on its hood, shattering its headlights, gnawing at the windows to try to get to the tasty morsels within.

JD tried again to make himself a more tempting target.

"Come and get it, you toothy motherfuckers!" he shouted, jumping up and down with as much vigor as his ankle would allow.

It was no use. In the culinary world of the suckers, he was nothing but a shit pie.

He could run. He was no match against an army of those

things. Why throw his own life away? Shouldn't someone live to warn others?

The instant he gave room for those thoughts, he realized they weren't actually his at all. They were his father's. If old Roger were here right now, he'd turn tail and run. And justify his actions until his dying day.

Well, Dad, since this might be my *dying day, I think I'll listen to Rowdy instead of you.*

"Friends don't give up on friends," Rowdy had told him. And he was damned if he wasn't going to pay heed.

A sucker version of a cheer rose from the monstrous crowd—all hisses and snaps and snarls—as they tipped the Ram onto its side. Chester hit the gas, and the tires spun, but to no avail. And when the clawing collective rolled the truck onto its back, it was as vulnerable as an upside-down tortoise.

JD tossed aside the now-useless T-shirt canon and readied himself for a kamikaze run.

It's amazing when inspiration strikes. And it does strike —there's no ambling or sashaying about it. Good ideas knock with fists of lightning.

JD stared down at the Mach-9 Multi-Launch—at its CO_2 canister, to be precise—and felt the idea thunder in his head.

He divested himself of beer bottles save for two, one for each hand. Hesitation had cost Chester and company the upper hand; he wasn't about to make the same mistake.

JD raced straight for the Airstream. Although his ankle sang in big operatic waves of pain, he paid it no mind. If he was right, it wouldn't be bothering him for long.

By the time he made it to the camper, the creatures were rocking the Ram back and forth. If they kept it up, it was only a matter of time before the strain would shatter the windows.

Before slipping inside the Airstream, JD took one last glance back to see if he could spy Trudy through the jumble of bodies, but he could barely make out the Ram itself, so thick were the suckers.

He stepped inside and slammed the door closed.

The Airstream had been well-ventilated by scores of mouths. He hoped it wouldn't make a difference.

When his good friend Trick was eleven, and he was nine, the two of them got picked up by the cops for setting fire to the field behind Carlson's Tap House. Their fathers were both inside—and had been for most of the day—and so they entertained themselves by playing a little game they called Hair Today, Gone Tomorrow.

The game consisted of trying to burn each other's hair off with hairspray cans Trick had filched from his mom's bathroom. They'd ignite the spray with a lighter and go after each other like the insane little arsonists they were. The result that day had been the scorching of Mr. Carlson's field.

JD aimed to play the *ultimate* game of Hair Today, Gone Tomorrow.

He set the beer bottles aside and quickly gathered all the nitrous canisters into a single pile in the middle of the camper. The few that had been leaking gas had all but spent themselves—his contact high resulted in nothing more than some mild giggling.

After ensuring he still had Rowdy's lighter on him —*thanks,* Rowdy—it was time for the entertainment.

He opened the cabinet containing the sound system and

powered up the stereo. He sent a little thank you skyward as the stereo's controls lit up a comforting orange.

The CD component indicated that a disc was already inside. JD cranked the volume up to ten and hit play.

He could have predicted what song would come blaring from the speakers. *No Fences* was his go-to album for years, especially on the road. And so when Garth started singing about his friends in low places, JD couldn't help but smile.

It wasn't long before the first mouth latched on. Another followed quickly, and soon, the Airstream was once again the place to be if you were a sucker.

The old camper groaned under the weight of the things. All JD could do was hope that the others would have sense enough to get while the getting was good.

He knelt before the hill of nitrous tanks and opened the valve of the topmost one.

Dear Lord, don't let me fuck this up.

He held the lighter up to the canister's nozzle and lit it up.

Garth continued to croon, and the tank continued to hiss, but other than that, JD's big sacrifice was an even bigger bust.

He lifted the tank off the pile and stared in horror at the warning label.

NITROUS OXIDE
MEDICAL GAS - RX ONLY
NON-FLAMMABLE

Non-flammable...
Shit!

TWENTY-FIVE

J D let the canister drop. It hit on the floor with a hollow clunk.

Flecks of metal and insulation fell from above as the suckers ground away at his Airstream. For it *was* his Airstream, in the end. Kate, who now no doubt sported a leech's mouth as well as a grudge, no longer had any legal claim over it.

He kicked the tank and shook his head. If only he'd spent more time studying in Ms. Demetry's science class instead of trying to figure out how to steal a nip of ethanol, he'd have known his big plan was a fool's errand.

If only Kate had worked for a big box store and was stealing propane tanks instead of jumbo-sized whippit canisters, he'd be in business. Instead, he...

Holy...crap.

He didn't need Ms. Demetry to help him figure out this conundrum; all he needed was Trick.

After the scorched field incident, JD and Trick had gone their own ways. Sure, he still saw the guy around town over the years, and he watched as Trick made the transition from being a pothead to a meth addict. But somewhere in between, Trick had taken to snorting whippits.

One of the last times he saw the guy was at a house party their mutual friend Dixon was throwing. Trick got himself kicked out not because he was high as a kite but because he'd popped one of his little canisters into the grill as a prank, setting off a small explosion and massacring a perfectly good batch of burgers.

JD looked down at the pile of monster whippits. All he needed to do was heat them up.

One of the suckers broke through the roof. It wedged its head through the ragged hole it had made, grunting and drooling blood as it tried to pull itself through.

JD grabbed up one of the two remaining Huckleberry Beers and flung it at the thing trying to birth itself into his camper. The bottle shattered next to its head, and the sucker made a rapid exit, screeching leechy curses at him. But as soon as it had disappeared, another took its place.

And this one, he knew.

Kate.

It had to be her, didn't it? Here at the end?

No matter. It was time to get cooking.

JD rushed over to the small four-burner gas stove set along the wall farthest from the door. The Airstream manual suggested turning the propane off during travel, but hopefully, being a fuckup would be in his favor this once.

The small blue flame that burst forth warmed his heart.

JD quickly shut it off and got busy.

He stacked four tanks across the stovetop. Then, he stacked four atop the first, perpendicular to keep the bottom canisters from rolling off, and continued this way until he'd completed a Jenga tower of nitrous. Finally, he leaned the remaining tanks all about the stove.

Sucker Kate screamed.

"Let's rock and roll," JD replied, and fired up all four burners. The sight of the flames licking at the bottom canisters was hypnotic.

A loud crash startled him out of his reverie.

JD whipped around.

Kate had gotten inside.

No...there was nothing of Kate in the thing standing before him. It had *taken* Kate. Its body was a map of mouths, peering from within the torn sheds of her scrubs, its pale skin etched with dark and bloated veins.

Another one of its kind dropped through the hole. JD knew there would be more.

He quickly backed away from his ex. His ankle, which had put up with him until now, had no intention of going in reverse. He stumbled backward and landed on his butt. Before Kate could pounce, he frantically crab-walked his way to the back of the camper and into its tiny bathroom, slamming the door shut behind him.

JD positioned himself on the toilet and planted his feet on the flimsy door just as Kate came a-knockin'.

The other suckers joined her, pounding, scratching, and gnawing their way inside, hissing and howling in their fervor. JD howled right back. Might as well make himself as lively a treat as possible to hold their interest.

So, this is how it ends for James Dean Speers, huh? Dying on the john like Elvis?

But, everyone got their ticket punched eventually, even

the King. The thought made him grin. Because *he* was king, wasn't he? King of the castle once more? For the last few moments before it blew sky high, the Airstream was once more his hearth and home. He'd gotten his boot back.

The first cracks appeared in the door, revealing the wall of teeth behind it. JD pushed back, legs quivering, arms outstretched against the walls. The thin material buckled, and he could *smell* them—their dead, fishy rot.

Teeth pierced the wall behind him. JD leaned forward on the toilet to avoid getting speared. Ravenous suckers, sensing him within, sawed away at the back wall, threatening to get to him first.

As the door's hinges gave way, the first of the nitrous canisters blew.

Squeals of anguish filled the Airstream.

JD laughed.

Not bad for a fuckup.

And then, the world lit up like the Fourth of July.

TWENTY-SIX

The lights in the VFW hall shifted from orange and yellow to purple and blue as the old disco ball, a time-honored relic of the venue, sent twinkling stars dancing about the room.

"A quick reminder that unless the owner of the blue Bonneville parked on the south lawn isn't moved, it *will* be towed," a voice on the loudspeaker said. "Up next, a slow dance for all you sweethearts out there."

JD placed his hands on Trudy Worth's hips as the cover band launched into a poor imitation of Rascal Flatts', "Bless the Broken Road." And when she put her arms around his neck, he knew he would never be this close to heaven again. Tonight, she wasn't wearing a dandelion corsage, and he didn't have crème de menthe on his breath. Tonight would be perfect. Tonight would be...

JD woke to a pain so sharp it nearly split him in two.

"Be careful!" Rowdy said.

"I'm trying!" Hailey snapped back.

JD pried open his blood-encrusted eyes. At first he saw

nothing but shadows, but as his vision returned, he found he was in the backseat of an unfamiliar vehicle. The smell of burnt meat was heavy in the air, and he had the distinct impression that a good dose of that scent emanated from *him*.

Hailey's face appeared in front of him.

"Hold on, I'm going to try again."

"Are you sure you know what you're doing?" Rowdy asked from the front seat. His buddy was fussing with the wiring beneath the dash.

"No."

"But you said—"

"I *said* I helped a guy relocate his shoulder once. That's a *lot* different!"

The woman gripped his arm—her hands felt cold as ice. Either that or his arm was on fire. It was then that JD noticed that his left limb had more joints that it should.

Hailey pulled on his forearm, and a nuclear bomb went off in his brain.

"Well?"

"I set one break, but his arm's still twisted like a pretzel."

Rowdy leaned over the front seat. He took one look and quickly looked away. "Whoa."

The door next to JD opened, and Trudy quickly slid into the spot next to him.

"How is he?" Trudy asked.

"He feels like shit," JD croaked. His throat felt like an ashtray, and he tasted copper on his lips.

"Try not to talk," she said, placing a hand on his head.

"How...?"

"You don't listen, do you?"

"How the hell did I...?"

"How'd you survive the fuckin' fireball?" Rowdy asked. "Damn explosion shot you outta that thing like cannonball. Walls musta been bitten down to Swiss cheese when it blew. Hell of a lot luckier than them sonsofbitches."

Rowdy nodded at the parking lot. It was littered with smoldering body parts—some still twitching.

Chester jumped into the front seat opposite Rowdy.

"Good of you to join us," Hailey said.

"Got it started yet?" Chester asked.

"Does it sound like I got it started?"

"Let's go, man! Who knows how many are still out there?"

Despite the pain it caused, JD leaned forward. A Hawaiian hula girl air freshener hung from the rearview mirror. That made the unfamiliar car instantly familiar. They were in Doc's old Impala.

"Red to red, then tap the brown together," he whispered.

"Huh?" Rowdy said, his hands deep in the Impala's wiring.

"Red to red..."

"Then tap the brown together," Trudy added.

Rowdy did as he was told, and the old car fired up. JD sighed. Some fathers taught their sons how to drive a car; his taught him how to hot-wire one.

Rowdy threw it into drive, and soon they were tearing across the parking lot with the road away from the Dockside stretching out before them.

"You saw how they reacted to my beer, didn't you?" Chester crowed. "That was freaking amazing. It's got to be the acetic acid content. Amazing!"

"Any chance you could wait until we're free and clear before stroking that little ego of yours?" Hailey groaned.

Chester held up a bottle of Huckleberry Beer. "People are going to want this. Hell, if this thing keeps spreading, people are going to *need* this."

"Is *that* the reason for the holdup?" Hailey snorted. "You had to rescue one of your fucking beers?"

"Maybe I could add a little nitrous, you know? A little callback from our exploits," Chester said, dollar signs filling his eyes. "I could charge whatever I want."

"Rowdy," Hailey asked, "would you mind?"

"Not at all," Rowdy said.

With his eyes on the road and one hand steady on the wheel, Rowdy hauled off and slugged Chester in the jaw. Chester's head bounced off the window and came to rest on his chest.

"Thanks," Hailey said, patting Rowdy on the shoulder.

JD was starting to wane, his vision dimming and becoming unreliable. Before he faded away completely, he felt Trudy's head close to his.

"If you pull through, Speers, I might let you have a do-over," she whispered. *"Might*, I say."

That 'might' was all JD needed to give in to unconsciousness. There'd be pain and questions and dealings with the law later, but for now...

The Impala sped off into the night, pines whipping by faster and faster as the survivors sought to put some distance between themselves and the Dockside.

And as JD slept, he spun Trudy Worth about on the VFW dance floor without a care in the world.

TWENTY-SEVEN

Barry Ward couldn't believe his fucking luck.

First, he'd struck out on the blackjack table. Then, he'd struck out with Monique, the cocktail waitress. Finally, he'd struck out with his choice of complimentary beverage. Huckleberry Beer? 'Suck it, Barry' Beer, more like.

He stood at the rail on the lower deck of the Delta Duchess Riverboat Casino, watching the sunrise paint the Mississippi a crimson hue, and flung the bottle of swill as far as he could into the roiling waters.

"Hey! Don't make me report you," came a voice from above. Barry craned his neck to find a man in a white uniform glowering down at him. Not the captain, Barry thought, but one of his minions. Lesser Assistant Captain Number Three.

Barry raised his hands in an innocent gesture, all the while thinking, *prick, prick, prick!*

He stared at the thundering paddlewheel churning up water and wondered what Mark Twain would think of his old riverboats being cannibalized and turned into floating Vegas wannabes.

Probably something witty. Something like…

But, not being a witty man himself, Barry couldn't conjure up a retort. Instead, he resigned himself to hocking a loogie into the great river.

His luck had to change. It just *had* to. Althea had left him, taking the kids, and his job at Tiger Foods was shaky, at best. One more write-up and it was the old unemployment line for Barry Ward.

He was about to go in search of a replacement beverage when he spied something angling toward the boat. The Delta Duchess wasn't the fastest thing on water—most patrons enjoyed the leisurely Sunday morning cruises. And so, when the jon boat appeared, seemingly caught in the Mississippi's current, it was no surprise to Barry when the small craft collided with the larger.

To call it a collision would be to give collisions a bad name. The jon boat tapped the Duchess, more like, catching itself in the boat's wake. Sticking close like a lamprey.

The deck on which Barry stood was a mere twelve feet or so above the waterline, and from his vantage point, he could see that there was a lone passenger aboard the little boat. He was about to flag down Lesser Assistant Captain Number Three when he realized who—or rather, what—the passenger was.

It was an old German Shepherd.

Wasn't there an old story about an owl and pussycat who went to sea? He guessed they'd have to write a new one now.

The scruffy mutt looked up at him.

Barry had seen fear in a dog's eyes before. Up close and personal. The hound his Althea had brought home for the kids one Christmas had been a nightmare—peeing on the carpet, on the furniture, in their bed. But he had taught that pooch to respect his property, oh yes, he had. And the fear in that dog's eyes let him know that *he* was the master of the house, not it.

This dog had none of that fear. Even though its situation was well and truly perilous, it looked up at him without a shred of concern for him or for the giant craft lording over it.

No. When Barry looked into the Shepherd's eyes, all he saw was hate.

And hunger.

As the dog leaped from the jon boat and scrambled aboard the Delta Duchess, its mouth painfully twisting into an oval of pure white teeth, which it promptly sank into his face, Barry could only think...

I can't believe my fucking luck.

ACKNOWLEDGMENTS

Special thanks to the Sorensen family, my beta readers (Nick Sullivan, Steph Hilliard, Leslie Farrell, Steve Stred), my amazing wife Debbie, and all the readers out there who seem to dig my stuff. A shout out to Michael Wormser (Cinemand Films) who took an early interest in this story back when it wanted to be a screenplay. And finally, thanks to Kathy Errington for her permission to place Frank's lovely quote atop this book—the entire horror community misses you, Frank!

ACKNOWLEDGMENT

ABOUT THE AUTHOR

Chris Sorensen is the bestselling author of *The Nightmare Room, The Hungry Ones,* and *The Messy Man.* He's penned more than a dozen plays for Thin Air Theatre Company and the Butte Theater of Colorado, including *A Haunting at the Old Homestead, The Vampire of Cripple Creek,* and *Dr. Jekyll's Medicine Show.* He lives with his wife and pups in the Garden State of New Jersey, where he splits his time between writing spooky stories and narrating audiobooks. Chris has narrated over 250 titles for Audible Studios, Tantor Media, Recorded Books, and many others. He is a member of SAG-AFTRA and the Horror Writers Association. When he's not writing or recording, you can find him haunting old bookstores and Indian restaurants.

ALSO BY CHRIS SORENSEN

Bee Tornado

The Nightmare Room

The Hungry Ones

The Messy Man

and

The Mad Scientists of New Jersey